DANCER OFF HER FEET

This book is dedicated to Tom

ACKNOWLEDGEMENTS

It is for all those little thoughts, gestures, words, letters, love, patience and understanding that I thank so many people.

Many friends and relations have contributed in different ways to this book, and I thank them.

Many doctors, nurses and hospital staff have my very grateful thanks for their care.

I hold an enormous special 'thank you' for Lucy (and her family) for unending patience, humour, support and understanding in the writing of my story.

DANCER OFF HER FEET

Julie Sheldon

with

Lucy Elphinstone

HODDER AND STOUGHTON
LONDON SYDNEY AUCKLAND

Copyright © 1991 by Julie Sheldon and Lucy Elphinstone

First published in Great Britain 1991

The right of Julie Sheldon and Lucy Elphinstone to be identified as
the Authors of the Work has been asserted by them in
accordance with the Copyright, Designs and Patents Act 1988.

10 9 8 7

British Library Cataloguing in Publication Data
A record for this book is available from the British Library

ISBN 0 340 54485 6

Printed and bound in Great Britain by
Mackays of Chatham plc, Chatham, Kent

Hodder and Stoughton
A division of Hodder Headline Ltd
338 Euston Road
London NW1 3BH

Contents

SCHOOL PRAYER

O Lord, take me,
All that I am,
All that I have,
And break me,
If it be Thy will,
To remake me
According to Thy will,
That through me Thy will
May be done.
Amen.

(A prayer used at Elmhurst Ballet School)

Preface

How quickly one forgets! A good friends of ours, who suffers from Dystonia, came round for tea. He isn't wheelchair bound but has quite a tremor and intermittent neck and arm spasms. And I gave him a cup and saucer to drink from. The tea slopped and spilt over as he tried valiantly to get the hot liquid to his lips. I kicked myself for such insensitivity – *of course* he needed a mug and straw to drink from – as I had needed before. And in such a short space of time I had forgotten! I vowed then to try and remember what it was like to be disabled. It was after all very humiliating to drink tea through a straw like a child. It was this, and other incidents, that prompted our involvement with the Dystonia Society.

My first reaction, on being freed from this awful illness, was to forget it ever happened and to rid myself of any reminders of deformity and disablement. But bit by bit it became clear that I couldn't keep this wonderful healing to myself. Over and over again the telephone would ring and letters arrive wanting to know what had happened, and always they would conclude, 'Your story gives us all such *hope* and encouragement.' Each phone call would bring another sad tale – not only of Dystonia, but all kinds of suffering. How did we have faith through such trials? How did the children manage? How did your husband find it all? And, of course, how on earth did you cope? The relief in people's voices when I replied 'badly' to this question was very evident, and seemed to be the trigger to start conversations of years of pain, suffering and inner hurts. When you read stories of how people recover from horrific times in their lives, it often appears that they sailed through blow after blow, but the reality, in *any* family, is that you often *do* cope in the moment of crisis, but after that has passed and you are faced with years of pain and disability, life can seem very bleak and lonely.

I sincerely hope and pray that as you read this book, especially if you are suffering or know of someone who is facing disability of any kind, you may be encouraged. I have been so fortunate in many loving friends and a supportive family, but also know many people who struggle on, seemingly alone. Even in the worst times of the illness, when communication was almost impossible, the one thing I hung on to was the realisation that *nothing* in all creation can separate us from the love of God, neither pain, suffering, disability nor even death.

1

Curtain Up

In the semi-darkness of the ward, a nurse stood watching. Watching not so much the form in the bed, as the screens, the dials, the scans and the monitors. There was little human sound, just the clicks and hums of machines – and a strange rasping noise like a dying animal panting in a trap. Beneath the tubes and drips and wires lay an oddly twisted and skeletal shape, shaking convulsively. From somewhere above the bed I looked down at the trembling, contorted figure with pity, but a strange detachment. That was not really me. I was, at that moment, and always had been, I knew, quite distinct from that broken body, crippled by pain and drugs. The real me was still free, free to know love, joy, laughter, free to remember, and free never to give up hope.

Even as I looked, the hospital scene began to blur and fade. A mist descended slowly over a dark lake and as the sun set, a white swan flew slowly out of the swirling shadows and alighted on the bank. As it did so, it was transformed into a beautiful princess. Alone in the clearing moonlight, she began to dance, but what a story of grief and anguish she seemed to tell. Every line of her body showed that her heart was breaking. Nearer and nearer she drew to the water's edge, and suddenly fear gripped me as I realised she intended to throw herself into the icy blackness.

I tried to rush forward to save her, tried to shout, but I couldn't move and no sound left my lips. Then, with a roar like waves crashing on a beach, the lake disappeared and I was back in the hospital ward. An alarm bell was ringing urgently somewhere, and the form in the bed was being thrown into hideous contortions by violent spasms. White figures were rushing and several of them tried to hold down the twisting shape as another gave an injection.

Gradually, quietness once more. And then the sound of a piano playing. The hospital ward faded again, and I saw a little girl in a pink leotard holding her mother's hand tightly. A door swung open on a studio which seemed enormous but the child wasn't afraid. Marching up to the tall, tall teacher, she announced brightly, 'I want to be a ballerina.' The teacher blinked for a moment then quickly resumed her air of authority. 'Very well,' she replied briskly. 'Get into line dear, and we'll see what we can do.'

I looked again and the little child seemed suddenly older, though the scene was much the same – a large mirrored room with a barre down one side, a piano playing, and the swish of ballet shoes on the worn wooden floor.

'Smile, girls, smile,' the teacher was urging, and instantly the girls' mouths opened in a mechanical smile which never reached their eyes. Their faces were glistening with sweat so that I couldn't tell if there were tears as well on their cheeks. Through the toe of one girl's ballet shoe, a tell-tale red stain was appearing. Still they smiled as they danced as if each movement was effortless, their limbs as light as feathers, as graceful as swans.

Swans. The exquisite white costumes, the haunting music of Tchaikovsky's famous ballet filled my vision once more. The swan princess was reunited with her beloved prince, and even though their future was doomed by the sorcerer's spell, their dance was full of hope and joy mingling with the sorrow, a song of the indestructibility of love. As the first rays of dawn tinged the downy dress of the swan princess with crimson, they leapt hand in hand into the waters of the lake, breaking the sorcerer's evil power for ever, united finally in a world of eternal love.

The music rose to a crescendo and then died away. As I strained to hear the last notes, I found myself locked once more within the misshapen body in the hospital bed, awake, finally, inescapably. My face was wet with tears but I couldn't lift my hand to wipe them away; couldn't walk, couldn't dance, couldn't even breathe or swallow without masks and tubes. Yet somehow, that dream or vision, whatever it was, had left me with something that wouldn't let me despair. The tears had dried on my cheeks now and I felt quiet and at peace, despite the ceaseless tremor in my body.

It was only five o'clock in the morning, yet a nurse came up to my bedside. 'The chaplain will be here at six to give you Holy Communion so let's get you ready,' she whispered. Very quietly and gently, she helped me into a clean nightdress. This took nearly half an hour for there were so many tubes and drips to negotiate and my body was now permanently curled up in a ball. It took a great effort to lever my arms against the contracting muscles and push them into the sleeves of my gown. Then the nurse changed the pillow-case and top sheet for freshly starched ones, carefully smoothing them out until she was satisfied. All the time I could sense her reverence for the occasion, and her gentleness with me in her preparations. She brushed my hair and arranged it carefully on the pillow, then brought a warm cloth to wipe my face. Hardly a word was spoken as the other patients were still sleeping, and she seemed so absorbed in making sure every detail was just right. She left me for a moment and returned with a little white lace cloth which she laid on a table she had found, and then selected a few flowers from the arrangement on my bedside locker. A bronze crucifix had also appeared and she gently placed the flowers at the foot of the cross. I was transfixed by her activity. She took a long look around, drew the curtains for privacy, and smiling, quietly slipped away. I felt totally prepared to meet with Jesus, calmed like a child, and so touched by this preparation.

The hospital chaplain arrived in his robes. He prayed very quietly and gave me the bread and wine. It took less than a minute; the preparation had taken an hour. Yet it was the most profound communion I have ever received. Even my body seemed to be stilled by the sense of God's presence. The tremors grew less and my breathing easier. My mind felt clearer than it had for months. As I lay there, drinking in the warm sense of God's love, so many incidents in my life came flooding back, and my thoughts returned to how it had all begun.

There are times in our lives when our destiny seems so sure, when every element of our future seems laid bare and unquestionable, as distinct as pebbles on a beach, washed bright after the tide. So, at the age of three, in that first ballet class, when I marched up to the teacher and announced that I wanted to be a ballerina, my conviction that I would succeed seemed to me simply a matter of fact, not of aspiration. It wasn't conceit, nor the result of family indoctrination; merely an observation.

Miss Rouse was a rigorous teacher but I loved every minute of her classes. It was like a new birth. Dancing seemed my natural instinct. The movements were pure joy, the discipline something I positively welcomed, and the early exams supremely exciting rather than frightening, an opportunity to stretch myself further, to do my utmost to please my teacher. Then, suddenly, it was as if a tide turned and all at once my destiny seemed to become shapeless and uncertain. When I was six years old, I developed glandular fever, and the energy which had fired me with such a passion for dancing was replaced by a painful, dragging tiredness, and I suffered months of lethargy and weakness. Dancing was out of the question. To lift my spirits and provide an interest in the great emptiness that was left in the long days of convalescence until I could start dancing again, my parents gave me a pony. As I grew stronger, so my interest grew and grew, until riding, too, became a passion.

We were living in an old farmhouse in a pretty Devon village near Plymouth, a home with outbuildings and a garden ideal for the menagerie which I, with my sister and two brothers, gradually gathered around us – Twinkle the rabbit, Higgins the Mina bird, Freddy the tortoise, Tickle the kitten, Gayle my little grey pony, then Pip, a bay, and later Peekaboo, a larger black Dartmoor. I toured the gymkhanas, and passed wild, glorious days with the Dartmoor Hunt, wind in my face, and pockets stuffed full of fruit gums. My mother was a keen horsewoman, and the hours of preparation for shows — plaiting manes, shampooing tails, oiling hooves, loading ponies into trailers — and sharing triumphs and failures drew us very close together. Rows of bright rosettes filled the tack room.

The real satisfaction was not simply in the winning, but in the very act of showing. I loved the theatricality of dressing up, whether in hunting stock and bowler, or as a mermaid in the fancy dress. I revelled in the pleasure of performance, in the beauty of harmony and balance between pony and rider.

So my early childhood passed in happy, even idyllic, fashion. We all but lived outside, tearing around on bikes in the stable yard, building dens in the garden, swimming in the sea, rambling on the moors searching for bilberries, picking flowers along the beautiful Devon banks. We loved messing about in boats on the River Yealm with my father, a keen sailor. When the weather closed in, as it can so uniquely in the West Country, with a clinging mist and steady drizzle so that we couldn't even see the garden, let alone the hills, we would play in the attic, make believe games and dressing up, acting our own plays and performing our own dances and songs.

Our year was punctuated with holidays, usually to my father's mother and step-father (to Gan Bayliffe's, we called it) in Cornwall. These holidays were spent in glorious Swallows and Amazons-style: boating on the Helford River, swimming in the beautiful Cornish coves, or searching hopefully for oysters as if they were Spanish treasure on Port Navas beach. Later on we became more adventurous as a family, and set off for a chalet overlooking Lake Thun in Switzerland. Each morning we children would go to the local farm and fetch milk in cans from the nodding, large-eyed cows with their huge mellow bells tinkling as they swung sedately into the yard.

My parents had four children in fairly quick succession, Nigel, Annie, me and Alec, and apart from the fact that Annie and I persecuted our poor older brother unmercifully, we were a very close and happy family. My parents married in 1952 after a blind date at a summer tennis ball and a whirlwind romance, becoming engaged just four weeks after their first meeting.

Mother comes from a family which combines a strong artistic and intellectual tradition (her own mother was a dancer, and her brother went on to become the well-known actor Alec McCowen) with the heavy Victorian influences of hard work and religion – this latter from her father's family. Her father built up several successful retail businesses in Kent and Sussex, but he may be more remembered for his somewhat eccentric religious convictions, and the setting up of a Ministry of Christianity in Whitehall during the War. At the same time he was down-to-earth and passionate, given both to rages and extravagant demonstrations of affection. In such an atmosphere, my mother's upbringing was colourful, if slightly unconventional. She was the apple of her father's eye, and feels her childhood was a very happy one.

But my father was less fortunate. He adored his mother, an accomplished pianist, but stood in fear of his father, a determined and powerful businessman. Chairman of a group of companies throughout Devon and Cornwall dealing in coachbuilding and agricultural engineering, his father had little time for his wife and child. The inevitable divorce when their son was just nine years old was painful and traumatic, and my father was sent off to a prep school blessed with an alcoholic headmaster. Brought up by his father, largely separated from his mother, he was drilled to take his place in the family business, and placed under constant pressure to be tough and to succeed – but never to steal the limelight from his autocratic father.

This strain was the only real cloud to darken our skies as children. My parents had to put up with frequent changes as my father was sent to different courses and firms in his grooming for higher management. Yet maybe all the pressure had an unforeseen benefit which was to have far-reaching effects in years to come. As his father placed more and more emphasis on material success and financial gain, so my father began to find deeper meaning in spiritual things. It was my sister, Annie, who unwittingly sparked it all off. While my parents had always been nominal believers, our bedtime Bible stories, read by my mother out of the big book won as a Sunday School prize, had always been a matter of habit rather than deep conviction. Interspersed with fairy tales and other children's books, their significance probably escaped us all, so it came as a strangely poignant challenge when Annie asked innocently, 'Are these stories really true, Mummy?' 'Of course, darling,' my mother replied quickly, but there was colour in her cheeks and she wouldn't meet our eyes. We were put to bed early that night.

It was of little importance to the four of us at the time, but for my parents it was a turning point. They felt they had to know for themselves whether the stories *were* true, and if so, what difference that should make to their lives. A growing desire for a personal faith in God led to their joining the local church and gradually finding a deep and sincere Christian conviction. A sense of God's love and reality quietly spread through the whole family, and gave us all, I think, an inner strength we were hardly aware of as children.

My parents, however, soon needed that inner strength. My grandfather's firm had been expanding steadily, and my father had been responsible for a large building development for the business. He himself organised the opening ceremony of one of the agricultural complexes, and personally shook the hands of the four hundred people who attended. But his father refused to appear. He couldn't bear to be upstaged by his son, to witness the success of someone else in his own business. His son, whose life's efforts had been to please his father, was deeply hurt. Only my mother knew how deep that rejection went.

Sometime later, at the age of thirty-seven, my father suffered two heart attacks within a fortnight. Months of hospital, countless doctors' visits, a heavy anxious brooding in the house when friends and relations called, left us as children confused and upset. Whatever desperation and fear she may have felt, my mother appeared to us strong and calm. In the middle of the crisis, something prompted her to phone the Bishop of Plymouth, Guy Sanderson, to ask him to come and pray. Significantly, from that moment my father improved steadily. But eight doctors independently advised him that he shouldn't go back into the family business, and for two years he was off work completely.

With the breadwinner unable to work, I had to leave my private school in Plymouth and come back to the village primary school when I was eight. This move, to me, was not without benefits as it gave me more time to ride my pony, run wild on the hills, and get away without working so hard. But it didn't last long. Two years later I was sent off to the Notre Dame Convent prep. school in Plymouth with Annie, and here All Things Were Taken Seriously. Happily they thought dancing was important too. My modest weekly ballet lesson, meanwhile, was leaving me hungry for more. Soon I was having several lessons a week and the exams seemed to fly past. Month by month, my old conviction grew that I would one day be a ballerina.

If there had ever been any doubt in my mind, it was scotched for ever by my first magical visit to Covent Garden at the age of nine.

I was trembling with excitement as Mum and I walked into the foyer of the Royal Opera House after our long train journey from Devon to London. All around me pictures of the exquisite movements and costumes of Tchaikovsky's *Swan Lake* lined the walls. Mum squeezed my hand. I was wearing my best party dress and my hair was tightly secured on the back of my head in a ballerina's bun. Men in dark evening suits, ladies in glittering jewellery drifted past me. There was an air of controlled excitement and bustle. Then, after we walked into the auditorium, we both stood very still. It was like entering a huge and very beautiful cathedral for the first time – the same sense of awe, reverence and wonder. For me, too, there was the overwhelming feeling that this was where I belonged. This was the place, unknown, to which I had been travelling all my life. A lump came into my throat. Taking our seats in the front row of the stalls, we soaked up our surroundings, row upon row of red velvet seats, beautiful gilded tiers, the little house lights with frilled shades. Then the orchestra started tuning up directly below me, and I craned over the pit to watch the musicians in their immaculate black jackets and bow ties. The kind smiling face of a violinist caught my eye. He must have known it was my first visit as he gave me a welcoming wink. During the performance, whenever he wasn't playing, he seemed to lean forward to make sure I was enjoying myself. As if there could be any doubt about that! The inspired music, the enchanted world of the lake, the effortless, heavenly dancing carried me into a transport of delight until the curtain fell for the last time and I sat weeping quietly – whether for the fate of the prince and his lovely swan maiden or that my dream had come to an end, I didn't quite know.

That visit left a profound impression on me. Whatever it cost me, I vowed I would one day dance on that stage. I belonged there, I was sure, but now I knew what excellence was needed to earn that right, I redoubled my efforts at my dancing. I was faced with an agonising choice over my riding, for it is a fact that the muscles used in riding are incompatible with the ones needing to be developed in dancing. Sadly we sold my pony. It was just one of the sacrifices I knew I would have to make if I wanted to achieve my goal.

A dancer matures very young, and we knew that if I was to gain a place at the mecca of ballet, the Royal Ballet School, I needed to come out of the established education system and start at a special dancing school as soon as possible. It meant leaving my friends and my sister at the convent, and being away from the family for weeks at a time, but again I hardly counted the cost. There was no other way. The Elmhurst Ballet School in Surrey was one of the best, and to everyone's delight, I passed my audition and was accepted for a place when I was just eleven years old. The personal sacrifice, the hardships, the pain and the heartbreak of such a demanding and competitive career were never really discussed, probably quite rightly. Nor was the fact that only a tiny proportion of girls finally make it into a top professional career, or are able to keep dancing without severe or permanent injury. All these things would have seemed irrelevant to an eleven year old child. As we boarded the train to Surrey at the start of my first term, with a little girl called 'Muffin' who became my constant travelling companion and great friend, my excitement that I was at last starting out on the road to becoming a real ballerina outweighed all else. My feet danced under my seat to the rhythmic sound of the train. I have begun. I have begun. Here I come.

And here I lay. Helpless, crippled. Dying of an incurable neurological disease which had destroyed all those childish dreams. I squeezed my eyes tightly together to try and shut out the picture of that little girl bouncing excitedly on her seat in the railway carriage. Her journey seemed to have reached such a cruel destination. Would this intensive care unit provide the stage for her final performance? Indignity and agony in place of beauty and grace? With every failing breath I wouldn't accept this was meant to be my last curtain call. It was never meant to end like this.

2

Dance Of The Cygnets

Elmhurst Ballet School was composed of two main houses set in leafy grounds in the heart of rural Surrey. It took about a hundred and fifty girls from the ages of eight to eighteen and was renowned throughout the world as a premier establishment for the training of artistes for stage and screen. Its reputation continues today. The work in the lower part of the school covered the syllabus of the Public Schools' Common Entrance Examinations, and thereafter GCEs were taken, but by far the major part of our week was spent dancing or learning related subjects.

The Artistic Director, Bridget Espinosa, with a staff of specialised teachers, prepared the students for their work in the world of theatre. The curriculum included classical ballet, modern, national and character dancing, *pas de deux* work, costume and scenic design, history of dance, make-up, mime, repertoire and choreography. Girls also studied for the major examinations of the Royal Academy of Dancing, and for ballet as a GCE subject. Drama, music and singing were also taught.

Elmhurst Ballet School was founded in the 1930s by Mrs Helen Mortimer, a RADA-trained drama teacher, with a Miss Crisp who had a small school in Camberley. Mrs Mortimer developed the drama and brought in a Miss Helen Fischer as ballet mistress, thus creating a ballet school. Mrs Mortimer, whose artistic flair and dedication established the whole character of the school, died in 1958, and her son John took over the running of the school with

Miss Fischer in the same inspired, energetic tradition. He took on the role of school chaplain and became known as Father John. His wife became headmistress, and, since her name was also Helen (Mortimer), she was affectionately called Mrs John.

The school was run with rigorous but kind discipline under their dynamic guidance. The regime was strict. On my first morning I was appointed to kitchen duty with three other girls, which involved getting up half an hour earlier than the others and making toast for the whole school under an enormous old gas grill. Each slice had to be turned with a long, long toasting fork. Faces red and perspiring, we bore it all with fortitude for there were distinct advantages to this labour – namely, more to eat. Our fingers dripped from the vast quantities of hot buttered toast we devoured as we worked. Other duties involved laying the cutlery on the tables, putting out water jugs, and, as we got older, operating the steriliser. Each piece of crockery had to be plunged into a trough of boiling water, a task of such danger that I expect it would never be allowed nowadays.

My heart was in my boots that first morning as I crawled nervously out of my old iron bed with its lumpy horsehair mattress (surprisingly comfortable – one could make a nice warm nest in the dip in the centre) and prepared myself for this unknown ordeal. It was a far cry from the comfort and security of home, and quite a shock for any eleven year old, but I soon got used to it. Kitchen duties were required from each of us for seven days every other week so we soon became almost military in this exercise.

The residential hall was called All Saints, and each dormitory of six or so girls was called after a saint's name. Generally we rose at seven thirty and walked down a tree-lined avenue across a playground and up to the dining room for breakfast at eight. Straight afterwards it was prayers in the chapel, then academic work until noon when we changed for ballet class into a black leotard with footless tights. We teamed this with white ankle socks and a black cardigan over what was called a character skirt.

These were full, circular, brightly coloured skirts made of any material we chose. We tied our hair up in buns and finished it off with a ribbon of the colour corresponding to our ballet class — red, orange, yellow or pink. Later on these classes were named after the famous *pas de quatre* of ballerinas in the great romantic era of ballet: Taglioni, Cerrito, Grisi and Grahn.

Then we danced — and danced and danced all the more as the years went by. An ordinary ballet class might be followed by pointe work, for which we had to wear shoes with blocks. Standards were high. By tea-time we were dropping, and our teachers would have been horrified if they had known that for the last half hour all their pearls of wisdom were competing with the all-consuming thought of the glorious sticky bun we were allowed at four o'clock. There were times when I think we would have killed for that cream slice or chocolate cupcake.

In fact we sometimes performed an act of unparalleled heroism over these sticky buns. At the beginning of term, each of the youngest girls would ask an older one, a girl who was particularly good at dancing or singing, to be her 'pash'. This was a sort of puppyish idolatry rather than the fagging found in some boys' schools. Hero-worship really. There were certain sacrifices we would make and errands we would run for our pash in return for their favour and help. One such sacrifice was to save our precious bun or our fruit from supper, and bestow it on our pash in the hope of untold beneficence. This was a marvellous system for the older girls, but of dubious merit to the poor little ones who then had to struggle through perhaps a syllabus class for ballet exams, or a rehearsal for a show before supper. After our meal, we ploughed unwillingly through our prep, our bodies aching with tiredness. Then we fell, exhausted, into bed with no time and little inclination for any recreation.

On Saturdays we had character dancing in the morning. The rest of the day was free. There was no structure to our leisure time, so we simply played in the lovely wooded gardens behind All Saints — the usual girlish games of skipping, ball, making camps, and pretending to be ponies (though with us it was probably ballerinas again). With the sun filtering through the trees, it was very peaceful, and as we floated and danced in the dappled light we felt quite ethereal. We were allowed to use the ballet studios at weekends, so very often, from choice, we went in to give each other lessons, choreograph our own little pieces, or perform to one another. We were tremendously keen and totally dedicated.

Apart from going to chapel twice, Sundays were similarly unstructured except for the statutory letter writing. This sudden relaxation of the intense pressure of the week led to a certain amount of high jinks, particularly as there was almost no sports provision in the school since games used the wrong muscles. I wasn't a natural law-breaker, but I did come from a family where a certain amount of mischief was considered fair play. So while on the one hand I loved the convent-like strictness and the complete dedication to dancing, on the other I was always on the look-out for an opportunity to have some fun. Not surprisingly, therefore, I soon teamed up with Amelia. From a highly individual and gifted family, Amelia was, I recognised, a fellow-rebel at heart, though she conformed as demurely as the rest of us most of the time. She had a very quick mind and wit and was a brilliant mimic and actress. I found her great fun.

We became life-long friends – and occasionally partners in crime. One wet and cold Saturday afternoon in late October, Amelia and I, bored and restless, found that the glass covering on one of the school firealarms had been cracked, exposing the black button. What madness possessed us I don't know, but we started to play a game called, 'Who can press the black button hardest without it going off.' I pressed it gingerly, then Amelia, then me, then Amelia again, both of us giggling into our hands as we egged each other on. Inevitably on about the fifth go, I pressed it too hard, and suddenly the air was full of the wild, terrifying sound of alarm bells. The whole building seemed to reverberate with the noise and from every door and corridor girls came rushing, some with towels round their heads caught in the Saturday afternoon ritual of hair-washing. People were running, shouting everywhere, and it felt like the most terrible moment of my life. For several seconds Amelia and I stood transfixed with horror, then I turned and fled down the corridor with Amelia hot on my heels. Where could I go, what could I do, where could I hide? I ran blindly with the other girls out into the playground. By this time the Surrey fire brigade had arrived, but already people were realising that it seemed to be a false alarm as not the faintest trace of fire could be seen anywhere. Amelia and I knew escape was hopeless, so, fearing the worst, we owned up to the dreadful deed. The telling-off we received from the headmistress was almost as terrifying as the alarm, but at least we weren't suspended and she gave us a second chance. I don't think anyone in school found our antics on that occasion very amusing, so Amelia and I kept a very low profile for a while. In fact we both became little angels of virtue (for a short time at least) and I somehow carried off the Junior Cup for Academic Work and the Ballet Cup. Such was my reputation for industry that I even managed, as Amelia wryly observed, to gain top marks in a test when I wasn't even at school. I wish success was always so easy.

As young dancers, our feet were of the utmost importance, and each term began with a ritual we dreaded – an examination by the chiropodist. At least, it wasn't so much having our feet examined that we disliked, as the fact that we had to go into his room one by one, sit on a chair opposite him and place our foot on the towel spread across his lap. As each girl came out of his room blushing and embarrassed, it became clear, when we conferred, that in lifting our feet so extraordinarily high in the air, he was actually looking at a great deal more than our feet. These were our suspicions, anyway, so thereafter we grew wise, and wrapped our skirts firmly round our legs so as to satisfy ourselves that the poor man's visits were considerably less interesting!

Such things are part and parcel of life in a girls' boarding school and weren't considered worth even mentioning to Matron or our housemistress. It would all have been put down to adolescent fantasy. Besides, any impropriety would have been hard to believe in a school where church played a very large part.

We went to chapel every day. As befitted a school of budding dancers and actresses, the services were very high church, almost theatrical – lots of incense and bells, solemn genuflecting and dramatic signs of the cross, from forehead to chest, shoulder to shoulder. Those of us in the choir wore grey tunics, soft black ballet shoes, and saxe blue veils like nuns. We processed down the aisle in pairs, hands clasped devoutly in front, our heads suitably bowed, moving like sleek panthers with our black pointed toes. To the hardened cynic, it might have looked like pure theatre, but for us it was deeply sincere, and through all this artistry we felt very spiritual. I loved it. The Sunday service was particularly moving. For many of us, pupils and teachers alike, no church service has ever since had quite the magic, nor stirred the thoughts and emotions so much.

Essential to the power and beauty of these devotions was the school chaplain, Father John. A very tall man, he was always sweeping round corners in his flowing black cassock, and mysteriously appearing about the school when we least expected him. When he left the room the air hung heavy with the bitter smell of his cigarettes which he chain-smoked. He was an excellent teacher and his sermons and scripture lessons were always lively, interesting and very amusing. As president of the Actors' Church Union, he was a dramatic and inspiring figure, with a voice of stirring resonance and exquisite diction. His influence on me has been profound. I think I owe my deep love of church music, singing, poetry and drama more to Father John than to anyone else.

Each year he was responsible for producing the Christmas play. This had been written by Father John's mother in her moments of anguish when one of her sons was killed in the Second World War. It was more an act of worship than a performance, and moved me deeply. The play depicted the Nativity but was staged rather like a Greek tragedy. Angels with coloured robes and outspread wings stood imposingly on pedestals at the back of the stage like a Greek chorus. The story was conveyed by a series of dramatic tableaux linked by symbolic dance and mime. The music was reminiscent of the haunting themes of Latin plain chant, and the atmosphere was heavily charged with a sense of awe and reverence.

In a dramatic change of mood, a crowd scene followed the birth of Jesus, and the colourful national dress and dance of many countries were represented in a blaze of joyful celebration. Suddenly the happy spectacle was shattered by the deafening sound of a nuclear explosion. The whole building seemed to shake. In my first performance I played one of the children in the crowd, and we all crouched terrified, unprepared in rehearsals for the realism of this moment. In the centre of the trembling mass of bodies stood the young Mary clutching her baby. A cloud of dust drifted mushroom-like up from the stage, and the piano began a slow descending scale. The lights grew dim.

All at once, out of the darkness a small child ran to the front shouting, 'We are His children, members of His Church – the Church He came to form, for which He died.'

The effect was so electrifying that many in the audience wept. That scene left me with a profound sense that even when we seem beyond human help, we are never beyond hope. Out of despair and disaster, God can still bring life.

After this proclamation by 'Youth', the Shepherds and Kings came to offer their gifts to the Messiah, and this scene formed a symbol of the whole ethos of Elmhurst Ballet School. The words of their speeches were deeply moving and became imprinted on the minds of each of us almost like a personal vow, particularly the declaration of the King carrying gold:

All the joy you gave to man, the riches of art, the beauty of movement and music, as representer of the Arts, I return them to the Giver . . .

From the day we arrived at Elmhurst, it had been instilled in us that the gift of dancing or acting had been given to us by God to learn and develop to bring pleasure to others for *God* and not for our own fame and fortune. This altruistic aim was a genuine and wholehearted motivation for all of us. We did feel tremendously privileged to have been entrusted with this talent, and this created a very happy atmosphere, and a complete lack of jealousy or bitchiness which, sadly, can exist in some theatre schools.

The highlight of our week was our lesson with 'Madam', Bridget Espinosa, herself a former pupil of the school. An internationally-renowned dancer and teacher who later went on to found the successful London Studio Centre, she was a most inspiring woman whom we adored and feared simultaneously. Larger than life, she wore long Indian scarves wound round her head, diaphanous, richly coloured clothes, dozens of tinkling gold bangles, heavy necklaces, and calf-length black patent leather boots. Her gestures were as flamboyant as her clothes, and her voice was resonant and rich like an Italian opera singer. We were always nervous as we dressed for her class; Madam, after all, was responsible for our progress through the school, personally overseeing who was entered for which exam, and choosing the girls she felt showed most promise for the main parts in her yearly shows.

These productions were highly acclaimed and were certainly the most wonderful experiences for us. Performing on the stage was, after all, the very purpose of all our training: every time we danced there we had the feeling this was 'the real thing'. Since this was a theatrical as well as a ballet school, agents often came down from London to 'spot' budding young actresses for TV and films. Hayley Mills, Jenny Agutter and Fiona Fullerton had all been recently 'discovered' at Elmhurst. The summer show, in particular, was the flagship of the school. Professional by any standard, it was choreographed and produced by Madam Espinosa herself, with the help of other extremely good ballet and drama teachers. I was fortunate enough to be given some excellent parts in these shows. As we got older, a boy was imported so that we could dance *pas de deux*. It must have been awful for him, the poor chap, the only male among all those giggling girls, but for us it was tremendous. The show ran for several days and was attended by audiences from far and wide.

Our whole life at Elmhurst was characterised by this intensity of feeling and experience. Everything we undertook had to go beyond the boundaries of normality into the realms of excellence. Mediocrity could not be tolerated. We were pushing our bodies to perform movements they were never designed to do.

'Unless it hurts, you're not doing it correctly,' was a familiar phrase used by our ballet teachers. From the beginning, we became used to constant pain, muscles crying out from over-stretching, feet and toes bleeding from being pushed into ballet shoes that were at least half a size smaller than our normal shoe size. Tears flowed daily until we learnt that this suffering was necessary in our quest for physical perfection. What joy when a step was executed correctly and acknowledged by praise from Madam!

To the outsider it might seem as if children at such schools must be held there by parental ambition. But, paradoxically, the very suffering increased our determination to succeed. It also created a strong sense of unity for this was a communal struggle, as well as a personal one, for the highest of goals. We were all a long way from home, but together for the same reason: we were going to be ballerinas.

As the terms passed, I began to realise just how much ballet must take over every area of my life, but I only became the more determined to be a dancer. Not only was sport forbidden, but sunbathing was also out of the question as a dancer should look pale and ethereal at all times. There was great emphasis on our physical appearance; our body was the tool of our trade. Long legs, long neck, high insteps (we often lay for half an hour with our feet wedged under the studio piano to encourage a higher arch), and, above all, a thin child-like figure, preferably with a flat chest – these were the coveted features of the great dancer. Our hands were vital, too, as even if our face didn't betray the strain, our hands could. There wasn't one part of our body that didn't matter. A dancer has a definite 'look', so the oval face, good hairline, big eyes full of expression, straight teeth with a pleasing smile, were all cultivated or envied. And above all, we had to smile. The public don't want to know about the pain. Smile. They will be paying good money to watch you perform. Smile. They want to see beautiful lyrical movements. Smile. You must feel the music with every ounce of your being. Smile. Your arms must be soft and floating, even when your feet are doing complicated steps. Smile. Jump higher, stretch further, neck longer, hands relaxed. Smile. We became very good at smiling and not betraying the pain that our bodies were enduring. This was to be my enemy in later life.

But whatever the successes and excitements of those days, such intense pressure must take its toll. Several girls found the strain too much, and eventually left. Illness and injury were common. The striving for physical perfection, the sylph-like figure, meant that anorexia was almost inevitable, and its influence was insidious and infectious – I, too, was pulled into its net. A group of us decided to give up potatoes for Lent, and as they didn't seem too difficult, we thought we would see if we could give up other things as well – just for fun, really. The food at school was dismal anyway. It became a joke to see who could eat the least in a day. We became thinner and thinner but that was more desirable for a dancer anyway, so the teachers didn't interfere. Fortunately for my friends, they either got bored of the joke or realised what was happening and started to eat again in time, but by then I found myself unable to eat, sickened by the very thought of food, until, at last, I was too weak to be able to dance. If I hadn't pushed myself so hard and refused to let anyone know how I felt, I know the problem would not have gone so far, but I never let my parents know in my letters (in fact I didn't really think there was a problem), and my performance in class was always up to standard until right at the end. Then there was a flurry of concern, and I was sent ignominiously home, feeling rather foolish and wondering how my parents would react.

At home I found a haven. My mother made no fuss at all, but on the first beautiful sun-filled morning busied herself preparing a most delicate and irresistible lunch. Then we sat together in the garden and nibbled and talked, and talked and ate, and as the shadows lengthened, I poured out all my thoughts and fears and hopes until everything seemed simple and safe once more. Love and time were all I needed. In the security of my family, I could just be myself and there was no pressure to achieve anything. For some weeks, I rested and grew strong again – and, unexpectedly, learnt a great deal more about life and people.

My parents had left Devon after my father's illness, and in June 1970 had taken up a post as houseparents of Stagenhoe Park in Hertfordshire, a beautiful Georgian mansion acquired by the Sue Ryder Foundation as a holiday home for Polish survivors from the Second World War concentration camps. Built in 1742 for the Earl of Derby, it had been used during the war as a maternity home for London evacuees. Two thousand babies were born there.

After it was taken over by the Sue Ryder Foundation in 1970, about forty Poles would come for three to four weeks at a time. They lived with us like a huge extended family. These were people who were scarred both physically and mentally yet our involvement with them was one of the greater privileges of our whole lives. Though they had sacrificed everything, somehow they still loved God and retained an extraordinary warmth in their sadness.

These Poles loved children, many of them having lost their own in the horrors of the camps, but they had terrifying memories of the savage dogs in the hands of the Nazis. We could only keep a very small dog at Stagenhoe. They spent hours talking, hugging and playing with us, showering us with beautifully dressed Polish dolls, carved wooden boxes and trinkets which they had salvaged from the holocaust.

My mother cooked for them all – and cleaned, washed, ironed and shopped. It was therapeutic for me to help out with such mundane jobs, whilst my own problems were soon put into perspective by learning of the horrors they had endured. Term was almost over so I didn't go back to school for many weeks. During the holidays, Annie and I served meals, cleaned rooms and made mounds of sandwiches. My parents and a few others were paid three pounds per week, but dozens of volunteers turned up out of the blue to help during the time we were there. Everyone joined in the daily tasks. Sometimes the Poles would break spontaneously into song, filling the house with stirring melodies of their homeland which had sustained them in the concentration camps. Often I would put on my little white tutu and blocked pointe shoes, and dance to the waltzes and mazurkas of their native Chopin, the Polish colours of red and white ribbon flowing from my hair. At Christmas we children wrapped up gifts which had been donated for each one of them, thick socks and a packet of razor blades for the men, mohair shawls and soap for the women. Their joy and gratitude moved me deeply, the more so after I sneaked into my father's office and discovered their case histories and read about the torture and deprivations they had suffered. That people could go through such agony and still believe in God's love influenced me profoundly and gave me an example of courage and patience I wondered if I could ever possess.

Little did I know what lay ahead. It was just as well. Any obstacles that had come my way until then I had been able to overcome by sheer determination and strength. It had left me with a positive, optimistic approach to all that I did. But things started to change. Looking back over the events of the next few years, I feel there is almost a sinister aspect to events which at the time seemed random and insignificant.

Back at school, one of my teachers suggested casually that if I carried my books and school bag in two hands rather than one I wouldn't lean quite so much to one side. It was only a small tilt but because we spent half the day dressed in a leotard, it hadn't escaped the eagle eye of the ballet mistress. When the problem failed to clear up I was referred to an orthopaedic consultant. I went to the appointment with my mother and both of us felt that it was all rather a fuss about nothing. I wasn't in pain and it didn't affect my dancing, so my heart seemed to stand still when the specialist looked grave after the examination and X-rays.

'You have a curvature of the spine, I'm afraid. There's nothing really we can do to correct it, but if you look after yourself, it may not cause you any problem at all in later life. However,' he continued, looking even more serious, 'I'm very sorry, but if you carry on with your training as a ballet dancer, you will be confined to a wheelchair by the time you are thirty.'

A wheelchair? Disabled? My mother and I looked at each other in horror and then disbelief. Surely he had made a mistake, was overstating the case. But the doctor was adamant. There was a serious weakness in my back which it would be dangerous to aggravate. Numbly we left his room.

It was a very difficult decision for my parents. Should they insist I gave up dancing? But they knew it was my whole world. I couldn't conceive of doing anything else. And what if the doctor was wrong? I looked so fit and well now. In the end we rather shelved any decision. As long as it was causing no real problem we might as well carry on. Besides, I was certainly not going to let anything so apparently insignificant prevent my being a dancer. Nothing would stop me reaching the top. I put the interview out of my mind and danced even harder. But I never dreamt how prophetic his words would be.

The pace was hotting up at school. I was fourteen and for an aspiring dancer that is an age of decision. O level course work had been started and careers were being talked of, but the most important object on the horizon was the Royal Ballet School – the ultimate goal, symbol of golden opportunities, the hallway to fame. As a prelude to auditioning for a coveted place, we all needed more experience in stage performance and here the numerous productions at school gave us valuable practice.

But then things started to go wrong. First a persistent ganglion on my wrist had to be operated on. Then a niggling tummy ache turned into acute appendicitis. After the operation the wound became infected and developed an abscess. For nine weeks I was in a lot of pain, often with a fever, and in and out of hospital. But the real agony for me was that I had landed a star part in a production which we were taking to Illinois University in the USA. It was my first big break and I couldn't bear to miss it. Despite the pain, I managed to convince everyone I was well enough to go, and somehow I managed to get through the performances, but I don't think I really shone. In fact I probably looked grey and haggard most of the time despite the statutory smile. For me it was a wonderful opportunity that I just couldn't take advantage of, but I tried not to let people see my disappointment.

I had just started to get back to full health when disaster struck again. Late for a class, I was running along a corridor, and flung myself at the heavy fire door at the end. As I paused at the top of the long flight of stairs to hitch up my satchel, the door swung back and hit me from behind. Down I fell, hitting my head on the stairs and again on the stone floor at the foot. Terror, pain, then blackness. It was four hours before I recovered consciousness in a hospital bed, my parents sitting anxiously at my side. Despite there being no fracture to my skull, I was badly bruised and shaken, and it was some weeks before I was able to dance properly again.

I was determined to make up the lost ground. I practised longer, pushed myself further, absorbed every word my teachers uttered. The days passed in pools of pain and perspiration but I refused to let up. At last my efforts seemed to be paying off. It was a great honour to be picked by Madam as the model for an exhibition of ballet she wanted to give to a conference of teachers at the Lyceum Ballroom in London. The two lectures were a week apart and my mother and I wrote them in the diary in large red letters. We travelled up to London on the train in a state of great excitement. At the Lyceum my heart missed a beat when I walked onto the cleared floor surrounded by a sea of attentive faces. It is seldom one has to dance to an audience made up almost exclusively of experts and I knew that even the slightest fault wouldn't be missed. But somehow I felt Madam's confidence and trust in me, and my body seemed inspired. The lecture was a great success and Madam Espinosa's praise was warm.

The next week, as my mother and I prepared for our second trip to London, we were interrupted by a telephone call. It was Madam. The lecture had been held that day as planned and why hadn't I turned up? My mother grabbed the diary in a fever of mortification. The big red letters reassured us that it was meant to be the following day, but had we written down the wrong date or had Madam herself made an error? It didn't matter. Madam had rung off impatiently, leaving my mother and me swamped by a deluge of feelings. I had got through a number of setbacks before, but somehow this disappointment seemed to symbolise all the frustrations and heartaches of the past months, and appeared like an omen of trouble to come. Hot tears scalded my cheeks, and without thinking, I burst out childishly, 'Everything is going to go wrong from now on!' There was no reply. My mother was weeping quietly too.

Resolutely in the weeks to come, we refused to talk of the incident, and I doggedly applied myself to curriculum work. Besides, auditions for a coveted place at the Royal Ballet School were just around the corner. Candidates for the auditions were chosen by Madam and we were practising intensively. About six of us were picked to go to London for the first round of auditions. These drew several hundred dancers from all over the world for sixteen places the following year. The audition consisted of a gruelling class from which only one or two girls in each were allowed to go on to the second test which was a thorough physical examination. I was thrilled to pass the first round. Now only the medical stood between me and the chance of a lifetime.

We were checked over like racehorses. We had to lie on a couch while our legs, arms, backs were measured, and our limbs pulled around and over our heads. The spine was carefully examined, and the slight curve in mine was noted but finally dismissed. Even our teeth were checked. I held my breath at the end of it all. Would I be up to standard? Had I passed? My mother and I could hardly contain our excitement when we were told I had passed and would be offered an official place in the Royal Ballet School in the summer of 1974. The tide of bad luck seemed to have turned. The dream of a lifetime was unfolding.

3

Broken Dreams

The transition from the safe and sheltered world of Elmhurst to the jungle of bedsit-land in London was not easy for a sixteen year old to handle. On the one hand there was the intense control and discipline of our classes at the Royal Ballet School; on the other, there was the total lack of any structure or restriction in our social life. It was a very unbalanced existence. From having all the practical aspects of my life catered for, every hour of the day organised for me and no responsibilities, I was thrown into a world full of exciting choices and new experiences, with no one to tell me what to wear, what to eat, what to do with my spare time, how to spend my allowance or what friends I should have. It gave me a heady sense of freedom a bit like being drunk, and I seized every new opportunity with enthusiasm. I think I grew up about three years in my first fortnight of arriving in London.

I was living in a house with six bedsits for Royal Ballet students looked after by a landlady called Stella and her boyfriend, Sugar. The Royal Ballet has an undoubted aura and mystique to the outside world, and we girls were regarded like a glasshouse of rare butterflies, much sought after by men for whom a ballerina girlfriend (or even several) lent a certain kudos. It was a very flamboyant world, and all of us consciously tried to cultivate a suitably sophisticated and artistic image. I carried round a packet of cigarettes in my handbag for days before I actually tried one as I didn't positively *want* to start smoking, but it seemed immature not to as many of the dancers within the School and Company seemed to do so. In fact, my first cigarette was purely for appearances. I suppose many are. Not long after I had started at the Royal Ballet, I got talking to a friendly and vivacious girl in the dressing room, and invited her back to my little bedsit for coffee. As we sat chatting, Jane asked casually if I would like a cigarette.

'Have one of mine,' I said eagerly, wondering frantically if I had any matches. Finding the ones I used to light the gas oven, we both lit up nonchalantly. It required all my concentration for a moment not to choke, but out of the corner of my eye I did notice that she seemed to be displaying a similar preoccupation. It was only years afterwards that Jane confessed she had never smoked either and had only suggested it because she thought I did.

Of course we were quickly hooked. Cigarettes and black coffee, that was what we lived on. The one thing we did try to avoid as much as possible was food. Eating once again became an obsession for us all. Now, more than ever, we *had* to be thin. Our bodies were growing into full womanhood, but we were required to look like children. For some girls, the worst word they could think of was cellulite. The trouble was that dancing and exercising for more than eight hours every day meant we got ravenously hungry. So, many of us fell into the dreadful cycle of bingeing on cream cakes, chips or chocolate bars, especially on Saturdays as we sat for hours in cafés, and then starving ourselves for days in guilty misery. The main topic of conversation in the dressing room each day was what we had eaten, or how many pounds we had gained or lost. What a shame that in the supposedly noble pursuit of Art and Beauty we should be obsessed by matters so basic and mundane. In fact I was one of the relatively lucky ones as I stayed slim quite easily anyway, but the secret was to drink endless cups of black coffee which deadened the appetite and yet gave sufficient energy to dance.

Apart from Jane, I had found another close ally right from the start. In the canteen on the first bewildering day, I noticed a tall, strikingly dark girl sitting apart at a table with her mother. Pure misery was written on the girl's pretty face and I was feeling fairly low and homesick myself. I wandered over with my coffee and said hello. The girl looked up eagerly, gratefully, and as she returned my greeting I realised she was from the other side of the Atlantic. I could only imagine how hard it must have been for overseas students, so when Catherine's mother left, I introduced her to my friends from Elmhurst. Most overseas students were put in a separate class, but for some reason Catherine was put in the same class as me with only two other foreign girls. She obviously felt a little isolated so I stuck close, and we soon became great friends, sharing hopes, fears and pairs of tights like sisters. Little did I know that in just a few years she would marry my brother and we would indeed become part of the same family.

Jane, Catherine and I were soon caught up in the mad whirl of parties and dances at the weekends. We spent many a Saturday wandering around Kensington Market searching desperately for clothes to develop a suitably trendy appearance. At the same time, all the students of the Royal Ballet were regularly given free tickets to the Opera House in Covent Garden, and in complete contrast to our sophisticated image, we sat in wide-eyed wonder once or twice a month, just like children again, worshipping our idols. In our hearts, that was the world we really wanted to belong to, and, indeed, once inside the Royal Ballet School itself, we too were a small part of that magical world.

As we walked through the unimpressive door in Talgarth Road, the first thing we always noticed was the sound of the piano. Music was part of the very air we breathed, and I developed a passionate love of music, particularly classical, which remains with me just as strongly today. For our own classes, the unlikely Cyril was the pianist, and we owe him a great deal. Cyril was inspired. Cyril was Tchaikovsky, Debussy, Bizet in turn. The piano sounded like an orchestra when he played, and it made a significant difference to the quality of our dancing. We were also fortunate in our teachers, for amongst them we had the famous Julia Farron, one of the best teachers in the world. And one of the most strict. She conducted classes with the military discipline of an army general.

'You need to relearn everything,' she told us with energy on the first day. 'It's like tidying a chest of drawers,' she went on briskly, 'you need to take everything out first, and you may find it gets worse before it gets better.' How right she was. In the early days we often wept with frustration as well as pain.

We were under enormous pressure at the Royal Ballet School, and yet we loved it, for each day was so stimulating and exhilarating. The discipline of the work was intense, and we trained until our bodies were dripping with sweat and every muscle was aching with tiredness. We went through at least two pairs of pointe shoes a week. The curriculum consisted of classical ballet, *pas de deux*, character dances, mime, ensembles and variations from the ballets in the repertoire of the Royal Ballet, Spanish Dancing, stage make-up and choreography. We also studied the Benesh System of notation, a sort of choreographic shorthand which enables the recording of dances and has become an integral part of a dancer's equipment. We were sometimes at the school until seven at night. No wonder, then, our social life, such as we had energy for, was sometimes rather wild. I don't care to remember many of the parties we went to. We played with fire, I can see that now. The innocence of my childhood seemed a long way off. In fact, I deliberately tried not to think of it. I didn't want to miss out on all the fun – which, I argued to myself, we needed as a break from all the pressure.

The work *was* highly demanding. Yet all the time there was the excitement of watching and learning under some of the greatest ballet dancers in the world, and the times we received an approving comment or mastered a complicated step were golden days. The Sadler's Wells Studio was surrounded by glass rather like a goldfish bowl, and out of the corner of our eye we would often spot some very famous ballet celebrity observing us with interest, for the Royal Ballet Company and the School shared the same building. On several occasions Margot Fonteyn paused to watch. These moments fired us with greater determination to push ourselves further, to reach for that vision of perfection and beauty these deities represented.

I had loved every opportunity at Elmhurst to dance *pas de deux* but there had not been many. A whole new dimension opened up therefore, when seven of us were chosen from the first year to start *pas de deux*, Jane and I among them. We worked hard at the lifts, and what began as sometimes a rather ungainly heave into the air, became gradually a movement of grace and strength. Higher and faster we flew into the air. We were becoming swans. The music swelled, and we were floating, flying, as light as the notes that soared around us. Then, suddenly, the music stopped. My partner's hands had slipped and I had crashed heavily, awkwardly, to the floor. Sharp pain flashed through my back, and for a moment I couldn't move. The class gathered round in concern, and the poor boy who had dropped me was white with fear and regret. But the years of discipline produce an automatic response in situations like these. Biting my lip, I forced myself to stand. 'I'll be fine in a moment,' I said lightly, 'just a bruise.' I tried to smile, but the pain was still snatching my breath.

The next day, the pain had eased enough for me to be able to walk more easily, but my back was still very stiff. However a check-up by the Royal Ballet doctor revealed nothing serious so after a couple of days' rest I started classes once more. Every movement was an effort but I told myself that my back would soon loosen up if I kept on dancing. Besides, looming ahead was the Advanced RAD exam, essential (we knew) in our struggle to become fully-fledged swans at last. It is a gruelling test, complicated, varied and demanding, and the pass rate is not high. I *had* to pass. I was *determined* to pass. I danced that exam with greater concentration and effort than I had ever known in my life. Oh the tension as we waited for the results; the joy when I learnt I had passed!

But there was a price to pay. The pain in my back definitely increased but the doctor still couldn't see anything fundamentally wrong when he examined me, and concluded that the problem was basically muscle strain. I couldn't bear anyone to think that I was being a hypochondriac so I kept fairly quiet about just how much it hurt. I didn't even tell Jane or Catherine. Anyway, there was something much more important to talk about which I wouldn't have missed for the world: we had been chosen to dance in the Royal Gala Performance in front of the Queen Mother at Covent Garden – with Rudolf Nureyev and Dame Margot Fonteyn!

Backstage at Covent Garden is a very unglamorous affair. The corridors are very narrow, with cold, bare stone steps, and the dressing rooms are cramped and poky, but the thrill of actually 'being there' far outweighs any disappointment in the surroundings. We were dancing excerpts from different ballets with Rudolf Nureyev and Dame Margot Fonteyn starring as top of the bill in *Don Juan*. In the studios at Barons Court we had been thoroughly rehearsed, before taking part in a couple of dress rehearsals at Covent Garden. It was not until this dress rehearsal that Nureyev and Fonteyn finally appeared, and our eyes were on stalks. The whole experience of being on that stage at last, fulfilling the vow I had made as a little girl of nine, was wonderful and moving.

My place in the corps was directly behind Nureyev as we snaked across the stage, and he was so close at times I could almost have touched him. It was hugely exciting being with such a legendary dancer, treading the same boards, and he really did appear to us almost like a god. We were in a dream. But the dream was shattered, and the god fell rather abruptly from his pedestal when he suddenly stopped the rehearsal and began to shout and swear at the conductor in English which was bad in every sense. How could he possibly dance at that speed? Was the conductor a fool or an ape? Could he not read music? We held our breath, expecting him to flounce off the stage at any moment and never return, but somehow the director pacified him, and we continued the rehearsal.

More was to come. When we were performing excerpts

from *Don Juan*, the Ballet School students were all dressed as nuns. At one point in the action, the nuns (for reasons quite beyond my understanding now!) had to bump hard into Nureyev. How does one bump into a legend? The first time, we just tapped him rather sheepishly. Tirades again. Was that meant to be bumping? He'd show us how to bump. (Two chaste nuns were promptly flattened on the floor.) Next time round we duly attacked him as if it were a rugby scrum. I hoped he was pleased. He certainly couldn't have complained again.

But nothing could detract from the wonder and excitement of the actual performance. We stood in the wings, our hearts fluttering as we listened to the orchestra tuning up; I think we each promised silently to make this the dance of our lifetime. We might never have this chance again. Here was our moment of potential glory or shame. We would give it our best, and hope that in however small a way, we would shine and please, and not disappoint.

During rehearsals the house lights had been left on, so when we danced on to the stage that night, it was quite a shock to be blinded by the blazing stage lights. Behind them hung an enormous void of blackness. But the atmosphere was charged with expectancy. We could 'feel' the people, sense their presence and appreciation, imagine the rows of red velvet seats, glimpse the gilded balconies and the ornate private boxes. The performance was magnificent; all of us danced as if for the last time, and Nureyev was transformed once more by the inspired, superb dancing which had made him so famous. His *pas de deux* with Fonteyn was pure magic. I wanted the evening to go on for ever, to prolong that marvellous feeling of joy and magnificence as long as possible. The final curtain eventually fell, however, and as we stood on the stage taking our call, flowers falling at our feet on a wind of applause, I looked up at the Royal Box and saw the smiling, gracious face of the Queen Mother. If my life had ended then, it would have seemed complete.

Back at the Royal Ballet School on Monday morning, three pounds and fifty-five pence better off for that performance, the princely payment to the corps de ballet, reality reasserted itself − and so did the pain in my back. My mother, who had come up to London for the Gala performance, had had enough. 'We're going to get this sorted out once and for all,' she announced firmly, and marched me off to a Harley Street specialist. Within a few hours, his X-rays pinpointed the problem. For seven months I had been dancing with a fracture of the fifth lumbar vertebra, aggravating the condition and causing possible nerve and muscle damage. Not surprisingly he was unimpressed by the fact that I hadn't had it treated long ago. I was clamped into a full body plaster jacket weighing one and a half stone and strictly warned not to do any exercise for at least three months.

I was heartbroken. There was a saying at the School that if you took one day off dancing, you noticed it; if you took two days off, the company noticed it; and if you took three days off, your audience noticed it. To miss three *months* of ballet at this crucial stage would mean a loss of fitness and concentration which might never be recovered, and on top of this I wondered if my back would ever again be strong enough for the demands of a full-time professional career in a premier company. The specialist had not been optimistic. I went back to the Royal Ballet as a spectator, but it was torture watching my friends progress, trying desperately to perform the steps in my mind. Clenching my fingers into my palms so that they nearly bled, I endured the long hours of teaching, vowing that whatever the cost, I would make up the lost time. The mental stress was compounded by the terrible discomfort of wearing the plaster jacket. The summer was blisteringly hot in London, and I felt I would go mad with the heat and irritation. Yet all the time, I felt I had to make light of it all. Don't make a fuss. Smile, girls, smile. But inside I was crying.

Where would I have been without Catherine? Even without my saying much to her, she seemed to know what I was going through, and in a quiet way was an enormous support. By then I had introduced her to my brother Nigel, on leave from the Royal Marines in Malta for my grandfather's funeral a few months before, and there had been an instant rapport. He was a dashing figure in his Marine uniform, with a tremendous sense of humour and style so it was not surprising that Catherine was swept completely off her feet. They started courting from that day.

The weeks had dragged past unbearably slowly, but now after nearly four months in that strait jacket, I was finally free. How wonderful, yet how odd to be able to move unrestricted, if stiffly, once more. But stranger still were the dozens of large moles which had grown all over my stomach and back under the plaster jacket. They weren't painful, but the specialist viewed them with a little concern, so I then had to be referred to another clinic where, for years, I have had to return for checks and to have the odd one cut off if it has started to look bigger or slightly suspicious. Still, I couldn't care less about a few over-size freckles. What was important was that I was free to dance once again. I just couldn't wait to get back to the studio and see whether I would be able to redeem the months I had lost. But slowly, slowly was the way it had to go, to my infinite frustration, and it was another fortnight before I was allowed to use my arms and legs properly in class.

My teachers couldn't have been more helpful. As I grew stronger, they arranged extra lessons for me, with the experienced and delightful Joan Lawson who showed me great patience and encouragement, and towards the end of that second and final year at the Royal Ballet, the School even offered to have me back for another twelve months. But in my heart I was facing up to a bleak reality. Something was lost, whether it was strength, co-ordination or suppleness, I wasn't quite sure. Despite working and working until I could hardly stand from exhaustion, I was having to admit that I would never be the prima ballerina I had always dreamt of – and I couldn't bear just to be mediocre. I hadn't gone through all that blood, sweat and tears just to be in the corps de ballet for the rest of my life. It was more than a disappointment; it was almost like a bereavement, and I found it very hard to talk about it with anyone, to let them see just how much it hurt.

It was hard for Catherine too. By contrast, everything was on the up for her, and I know she felt guilty about it even though I was truly glad for her. The relationship with Nigel was going well, and rehearsals for the final spectacular production of *Coppelia*, the culmination of all our two years' hard work at the Royal Ballet, were well under way. I hadn't been strong enough to take a part, and every time Catherine returned late at night weary and flushed from the exertions of the rehearsal I watched her face cloud with sadness as she evaded my questions and changed the subject. At the end of our two years together, I really tried to be positive and cheerful with her and all my friends as we discussed our futures. Many were going to the Royal Ballet Company, some to other leading ballet companies, one or two into teaching. Catherine herself went off to the Pennsylvania Ballet Company for the summer. I had never really imagined any future except with the Royal Ballet, and now it wasn't clear just which avenue I should take.

Encouraged by my family and friends, I did take up the offer of joining a small ballet company which opened with a production of *Les Sylphides* at the Brighton Dome. My career as a professional ballerina lasted just a few weeks. The company had to fold up through lack of funds and I was left high and dry once more. By now I just wanted to do something completely different, to get away for a while and think, and on the spur of the moment, I took a job as a nanny with a family in Brussels. It was like a breath of fresh air to get away from the pressures of Sorting Out My Life. As a sideline while I was in Belgium, I taught dancing to little children in a local ballet school, and I got a real thrill from seeing their pleasure and excitement. Perhaps teaching was a real possibility for me?

When I came back to England I was so glad to hear Catherine was back in London so we arranged to meet up in one of our old haunts in Covent Garden. She too was at a loose end, and we got talking about the possibility of forming our own company to do commercial promotions and modelling. We thought it would also be fun to try some disco dancing, which we loved, as a real change from the rigorous discipline of the past few years. We were both quite tall, sometimes a disadvantage for ballet but no problem for disco dancing. We had one or two contacts in that line and our enthusiasm grew quickly. By the time we got to the bottom of our glasses, Two's Company had been born. But before we could explore the practical aspects of our wonderful idea (that is, how we could make a *lot* of money as *quickly* as possible . . .) and set ourselves up in business officially, a less attractive prospect loomed ahead of me.

In the nicest possible way, my sister Annie was making me feel very awkward about something. She was badgering me to go to Motcombe with her. Motcombe, so she told me, was a country house in Dorset where Christian holiday camps for girls were regularly held. What a turn off! My social life in London was a million worlds away from that sort of scene, and I couldn't imagine anything more rivetingly boring than going back into a boarding school world of jolly hockey sticks and hot chocolate before bed. And a *Christian* camp. I was embarrassed, even a little ashamed, to think about God too much. Faith had played such an important part in our family during my childhood that I was quite aware He could hardly be pleased with my current lifestyle.

Not that Annie hadn't had her fling. She had always been hardworking, responsible and conscientious at her convent boarding school, and it was no surprise when she opted for a practical and vocational career in occupational therapy. But she wanted to take a year off when she finished school at eighteen, and landed the unlikely job of touring the Middle East trying to sell encyclopaedias for a publisher. Not the most lucrative or rewarding of occupations one would have thought, and I imagined her sitting on a dusty roadside with her books spread around her like an impoverished street vendor. Not a bit of it. Annie spent her time hobnobbing with rich Sheikhs, eating sheep's eyes, and living it up in Hiltons. No self-respecting Arab, it seemed, could be without an encyclopaedia on his shelf. I'm not sure, in fact, how prominently book orders really

featured in all this, but Annie certainly had lots of fun,
taking risks, and getting into several interesting scrapes —
all of which impressed me enormously (though it must have
given my parents a few grey hairs). Looking back, she says
she was always aware of a sort of guardian angel looking
after her, and certainly it seemed little short of miraculous
that she eventually arrived home safely.

After such an experience of wealth and the high life, it
was interesting that Annie soon adopted a more conven-
tional lifestyle. The year I left the Royal Ballet School,
1976, Annie started an Occupational Therapy Diploma in
Oxford. She soon noticed that one of the main 'student'
churches, St Aldates, offered a *free* lunch each Sunday, and
it seemed an excellent way of meeting people. (She did
reflect that the convent nuns would not have been very
impressed at her motives for going to church.) For a few
Sundays the minister preached on the need for a 'faith
for all seasons', a belief in God which was constant and
personal, the foundation of all one did, rather than a matter
of ritual or habit. Jesus was the key, she realised, to real
meaning and purpose in life. He alone could give fulfilment
and happiness in a way that money and glamour never
could. She soon made a conscious decision to commit
her life to God and a few months later discovered the
reality and power of the Holy Spirit. Ironically this
profound spiritual experience happened while she was
doing a holiday job as a maid with friends in a Scottish
sporting lodge in the middle of the grouse season. Yet
another brush with great wealth opened her eyes still more
to the emptiness of materialism, and left her hungry for a
deeper knowledge of the joy Jesus promised. No wonder,
after all this, that Annie was increasingly keen to share
these experiences with her sister. Annie refused to go to
Motcombe if I didn't go with her, so, very reluctantly, I
gave in.

I loathed it. Compared with the exciting 'adult' life I
was living in London, it seemed at first like going back to
kindergarten, and the only way I could cope was by nipping
out into the rhododendrons every couple of hours and hav-

ing a quick smoke. Horror of horrors, the girls had prayer meetings every morning before breakfast, and before they went to sleep, they sat on their beds and read their Bibles. I felt as different from them as if I had two heads. And yet, something got to me. No matter how rude or anti-social my behaviour might have seemed, everyone was so *nice*. There was an atmosphere of great caring and acceptance. Even if I tried to shock them, I think they would still have shown me the same love and kindness. Somehow the glittering, flamboyant life in London began to seem hollow and pointless, just an illusion of happiness compared with the peace and joy that the crowd at Motcombe had found in God.

There was a lot of singing. Hymns, choruses, the house was full of music. I couldn't get away from it, these girls *enjoyed* being Christians. This relationship with Jesus they talked about seemed to be so real, so exciting, that I knew I had never known Him in that personal way. 'Behold I stand at the door and knock.' I heard a talk on this verse one morning, and I knew then, with a strange quickening of my heart, that Jesus was wanting to come into my life. Yet I was afraid. I knew it would mean surrendering all my hopes, ambitions and desires to Him. Would I still be able to dance professionally? What did God think of success and fame? But what would my friends think if I stopped going to the wild parties and went to church instead?

But when it comes down to it, all these things pale into insignificance when you are faced with the great God of the whole universe, and His special tender love for you. One night we sang the familiar chorus,

> Turn your eyes upon Jesus.
> Look full in His wonderful face.
> And the things of earth will grow strangely dim
> In the light of His glory and grace.

These were words I had heard many times before yet that night there was a huge lump in my throat and I couldn't sing. Slipping out on to the balcony at the end of the dormitory, I gazed up into the clear starlit night. There seemed to be no one else in the world in that stillness, just God and I meeting at the very centre of creation. Nothing else mattered except that Jesus had loved me enough to die for me, and wanted to share His life with me. 'Yes, Lord,' I whispered into the night, 'please come in.' And just in case He hadn't heard, I repeated it about twenty times. Suddenly I was silent. Out of the heavens His love swept into my heart. A new feeling of excitement, wonder and reverence filled me as I realised without a doubt that Jesus was now my own King and Saviour. For a long time I just stood on the balcony, breathing in the peace and beauty of His presence. By the time I returned inside, everyone was asleep.

The next morning, instead of hiding, groaning under my blankets while the girls got up, I couldn't wait to read my Bible. Somehow I seemed to know that this wasn't just a boring old book any longer, but the living Word of God. He was going to speak to me! I opened my Bible at Proverbs and devoured page after page. It all seemed so relevant, so perfectly attuned to my problems and situation. It was difficult to know just how to break the news to Annie, and I actually tried to avoid her at breakfast, playing for time while I thought of the right words. In the end, of course, I didn't have to tell her anything. One look at my face, and she just threw her arms round my neck. 'Oh Ju,' she whispered, her eyes shining, 'I'm so glad.'

I was touched by her love, and returned her hug warmly. Knowing her sense of loyalty and caring, I could imagine how Annie had been praying for me in recent months, and especially at Motcombe, yet she had never pushed things. We had always been close, but from that moment there seemed to be a new dimension to our relationship. By the end of the week, I knew how lucky I was to have her support. To be honest, I was getting a bit apprehensive about returning to London. It was one thing to call myself a Christian in a spiritual greenhouse, but to survive amid the pressures and temptations of life in the Capital would be quite another. How would I reconcile my faith with the work I hoped to do? Here was quite a different challenge.

4

Dance, Dance, Wherever You May Be

When I got back to my flat in London, the world of Motcombe seemed rather like a dream. But the sense that I could talk to Jesus, that He cared for me and was interested in every aspect of my life, was no less of a reality as the days passed. I could see why Christ urged his disciples to go and tell the world the good news of eternal life through Him. And having found such a genuine sense of purpose and fulfilment since my step of faith at Motcombe, I couldn't conceive of parcelling that off 'for personal use only'. Yet I didn't want to ram it down my friends' unwilling throats. I reasoned in the end that if it was so wonderful, so dynamic, they could see this great change in my life without my having to talk that much about it. I began to learn, too, that praying for people can do a lot more good than hours of vain discussion.

So I didn't say much to Catherine though she knew that something important had happened to me at Motcombe. I don't know if I could have described to her just what happened that night on the balcony, but as we discussed plans for Two's Company, it must have been obvious that I was looking at work from a slightly different angle now. Suddenly she asked, 'What do you think God makes of dancing?' I laughed. 'I think the angels do it all the time,' I replied. But it was a good question and it set me thinking. Dance has many forms and functions, and it seemed to me at this point that the important thing was one's motivation and inspiration. Would I be dancing for joy or for money?

Hopefully the two didn't need to be mutually exclusive. Now more than ever, I felt I had been given a gift by God, and I wanted to use it for His glory. Catherine and I agreed to look out for promotional work, but even as we did so, I could see that at some time it might present me with a dilemma over its compatibility with my faith. But I would cross that bridge when I came to it. Let's see if we actually got any work first.

While we explored various avenues and contacts, I realised I had to do something to make myself useful. My mother, ever practical, observed that there was an excellent cookery course being offered at a college near home, and this, coupled with the prospect of being with my parents for a while, seemed quite a sensible proposition. I hadn't exactly acquired extensive culinary skills, and perhaps I should discover a little of life beyond Mars bars and Mac-Donalds.

Having missed so much time with my parents while I was away at school, it was lovely to be back alone with them now, without the pressures of dancing casting a shadow over all we did and discussed. My parents had moved out of Stagenhoe, though my mother continued to work there until 1979.

The spiritual search in my parents' lives had brought my father to the decision in 1976 that he should train for the Anglican ministry. He was working, by then, for the Spastics Society in Hertfordshire so his training took him to St Albans two evenings a week. On becoming a non-stipendiary minister, he was licensed as a part-time hospital chaplain at the Lister Hospital in Stevenage for four and a half years until he was eventually accepted for full-time ministry. During this time, my parents were fortunate enough to rent a beautiful old beamed farmhouse in Kneb-worth. With its orchard and wild garden, it was an idyllic home, and the perfect retreat for me to work out what I was doing with my life.

The cookery course turned out to be quite good fun as well as worthwhile, and I could dish up beef stroganoff with the best of them by the time I finished! I managed to get myself some work at the same time teaching ballet at the Gordon Craig Theatre in Stevenage, and also gave private lessons to a very talented young girl called Jo, in whom I saw all my own childhood dreams and aspirations. Meanwhile I went along with my parents to the church in Knebworth, and found a lot of spiritual life there, generated by the vitality and enthusiasm of the minister and his wife, Ray and Jill Lockhart.

It was Jill who managed to draw out from me a light I hadn't felt worth removing from its bushel. I had always loved singing, and am one of these irrepressible bathsingers; in fact, I sing most of the time without realising it. I had never had the time or ability to give it any further thought, but Jill, who had a beautiful voice, encouraged me to sing in the newly-formed music group during the morning service on the odd occasion. From there we began to discuss the possibilities of using dance in the service, and I felt really excited at this. I had never seen dance used as a spiritual tool before, but it all seemed to fit into place for me. In fact, I realised how extraordinarily similar it all was to the Elmhurst Christmas play with all its expressive movement and beautiful music. It seemed so right to worship God with my body in this way, and it was a really liberating experience for me to begin to express my love for God in a form which was so instinctive. Jill and I wondered how dance in worship would be received by the congregation of our little country parish church, but we introduced it gradually and quietly, and found a warm response from even the older and more traditional members.

All the time I was learning more about how God can change your life as you open up your heart to Him. Hearing Juan Carlos Ortiz, a famous Argentinian evangelist, in London, had a great effect on me, and made me face up to the fact that you couldn't be a Christian just on certain days of the week when you were in the right company. My faith in God had to be total and unconditional. Soon afterwards I heard Rev Harry Sutton and Cliff Richard at All Souls Church, Langham Place, and that really did fire me with the determination to be a Christian in the secular world and not just in church. In December of that year, 1977, I met Janet Randall of the Sacred Dance Group, one of the key people involved in establishing dance in worship in this country. She was an enormous inspiration to me, putting dance in its biblical context by explaining how in the time of David, for example, the singers and dancers led the procession of people with praise and thanksgiving into the courts of God to worship Him. Dance, she explained, therefore was a means of drawing people into the place of worship, of opening up their hearts to God by inspiring them to praise and thank Him. For the dancers, it is an act of worship rather than a performance, an offering back to God of the love and gifts He has given to them. As a result of Janet's encouragement, Jill and I sang and danced at an evening of interdenominational celebration called 'St Alban's Praise' held in the cathedral.

So much was going on in my life spiritually, but at the same time, possibilities began to arise to use my dancing in another way. Catherine and I had managed to land one or two contracts for Two's Company. The glitzy world of entertainment and the media couldn't have been in starker contrast to the quiet little world of dancing in Knebworth church. We did a modelling job for Dunlop, for example, who chose 'Ballet' for the theme on their calender that year, and set up shots of us in all sorts of exotic locations and costumes. Great fun, it was, and lucrative, too, for the short time it lasted. But the morals and language, which I had taken as the norm when I first came up to London, now began to jar a little. It was a big help, therefore, when I was invited along to a dinner held at the Arts Centre Group (the ACG), which drew together Christians from the arts and entertainment worlds to encourage them in their faith, but also give them practical advice about auditions and job offers. It was an inspiration to meet people who were dynamic and successful in the secular world and yet who maintained a living faith in Jesus at the same time. I was fascinated to meet Cliff Richard and Eric Morecombe who didn't seem to have any problems reconciling their work and their faith. If they could reconcile the two, so could I!

Poised, then, to take the entertainment world by storm, I was stopped in mid-flight by a car accident that left me with a whiplash injury to my neck, putting me in Charing Cross Hospital for several days. It seemed to mend without problem, however, but my mother's old Ford Escort was a write-off. The need to earn some money sharpens the mind wonderfully, and within a month, Catherine and I were rehearsing for a large promotional function at the Lancaster Hotel, Bayswater. To be sure of a crust, I also took a part-time job in a dress shop, and began teaching keep-fit. Life was hectic but I loved it. I even managed to fit in classes for myself at the Dance Centre in Floral Street. I also started to go along to Holy Trinity Church in Brompton and met many new people who helped and influenced me greatly. HTB had an exceptional music group called Cloud which comprised a wealth of talent in singers and instrumentalists. They had made several recordings, and their unique blend of subtle vocal harmonies and sensitive instrumentation was famous throughout the country. Penny was one of the singers, and although I didn't get to know her well until some time later I was very struck by the reality of her faith, her enthusiasm about God, and her exquisite voice. Another girl suggested the idea of linking a dance group with Cloud as part of the worship, and it was a concept which captivated us all. Cloud's music made one want to dance anyway, and their words were so expressive that they lent themselves perfectly to movement and mime. As we talked, prayed and tried out some ideas together, we had a very real sense that this was a venture God was bringing together. But to get any further, the clergy had to see it that way too. In September three of us danced with Cloud in front of a 'tribunal' of the minister, Raymond Turvey, Sandy Millar and one or two other leaders within the church. We waited nervously for their verdict. This was worse than a ballet exam. Then came their answer. Sacred dance, they felt, was a valid and helpful aid to worship, and if performed sensitively and skilfully would provide an inspiration to the corporate worship of the church. We could dance in an evening service as soon as we felt ready.

And so, sacred dance became an integral part of the worship at HTB. We chose blue flowing dresses and the dance was a sort of balletic mime. We rehearsed conscientiously and prayed about the dances a lot, because while we felt sacred dance could inspire and bless if done well, there can be nothing more irritating and off-putting than people galumphing about in front of the congregation without proper choreography or skill. It's a difficult balance, for, equally, too slick or 'clever' a dance, and attention is drawn to the dancers and not to God. As a trained ballerina, I had to be careful that the performance-orientation of my schooling didn't result in a preoccupation with pleasing my 'audience' rather than God. I was dancing 'before the Lord' first and foremost just as David did – 'with all his might' (2 Samuel 6 verse 14).

It felt strange, sometimes, spending a lot of time with church people, and then tuning into a completely different wavelength for my work. My stage and theatre friends with their flamboyant and hectic lifestyles came from a world which would have seemed quite alien to the ordered, disciplined lives of my church friends. Whilst *I* saw the good side of both, it seemed easiest just to keep quiet about my 'other life' to each of them, and adopt a when-in-Rome philosophy.

One escapade which highlighted this dichotomy was my short-lived foray into professional singing. Encouraged by friends, I had paid more attention to my music and had gathered the songs I had been writing since about the age of fourteen into quite a portfolio. Contacts of mine in the music business arranged an audition for me with a famous record-producer. Clutching my folder of songs nervously, I presented myself at his office, this mecca of the music business, overlooking the Thames, at six o'clock one evening. An acolyte showed me into the temple, an enormous room surrounded by gold discs and photographs of the 'gods'. At the end of the room, like a sacred altar, stood a majestic grand piano. A door opened and into the room swept the priest, the Buddha. Instead of the piano seat, I was pressed into the sofa and plied with gin and tonic. 'Wouldn't you like to hear my music?' I asked in a tone of rather desperate hopefulness. 'Later, later,' he went on, and his eyes roved with interest over my legs. I realised instantly that his mind was preoccupied with more than simply the performance of my vocal chords. How I ever managed to get off that sofa without serious consequences, I don't know, but I felt I would now do pretty well in that radio game, *Just a Minute* where you have to speak without a pause on dozens of different subjects. But my song folder remained unopened, and that little scene sadly put the dampers on my music career for a long time.

Still, my attention was quickly taken up by another audition, this time with Two's Company for the promotional campaign of the 'Superman' record. Our audition this time was held in the impressive offices of Atlantic Records in London, and lots of other young hopefuls were waiting in the wings for the chance of their first lucky break. Catherine and I didn't think we stood much chance, but to our amazement our routine won the contract – and catapulted us straight into the glamorous world of showbiz. Around the same time we were also chosen to dance at BAFTA for the Imperial Radio Awards and for several company promotions for Fisons, compered by the *Tomorrow's World* presenter, Raymond Burke. So, suddenly, our life was a whirlwind of activity.

Warner Brothers organised a very high-profile promotional campaign for 'Superman', and our job was to choreograph a routine to dance to the music. We designed our own blue lycra superman suits with red capes, and had great fun putting together a performance which was a far cry from the classical decorum of the Royal Ballet. For a few mad weeks we were treated like film stars, driven around in limousines, and swamped by hordes of photographers and journalists at the various clubs where we did our show, including the Lyceum and the Hammersmith Palais. The climax was dancing at the opening ceremony of the BAFTA Film Awards early in 1979, in front of the world's cameras and every famous face in the film industry. We did radio interviews for Capital, Luxemburg, Radio One, and I suppose we could have kidded ourselves that we had really made it to the top. But in this business you can be flavour of the month for a while, but it lasts only as long as you work for the big names. In yourself, you are worth nothing to the newshounds and hangers-on who flutter round like moths while you're in the limelight.

Though I really enjoyed all the razzmatazz for a while, I could see that the whole scene was really like a big, glittering balloon. There seems to be so much warmth, gaiety and laughter, but when the balloon bursts, there's not a lot left. I had grown up in the world of theatre, and was accustomed to all the extravagant talk and gestures. I also had my contact with the ACG, and some sincere friendships there. But anyone who set too much store by success and glamour often learnt the hard way that unemployment and obscurity were always just the end-of-a-contract away.

If the superficiality and decadence of showbusiness saddened me sometimes, the very conformity of church made me feel uncomfortable. My lifestyle was too unconventional to fit in easily with what I was still perceiving as the 'squeaky clean' image of the Christian girls I had met. So when some girls from the church offered me a place in their flat in Victoria (so convenient for HTB), I wondered how I could refuse without sounding rude.

It was my cousin, Sarah, who provided me with an escape route. Her boyfriend Peter, an insurance salesman had apparently been trying to persuade a chap called Tom to do business with him, and in a desperate attempt to change the subject (I gathered later) Tom had claimed an urgent need to find a tenant for his flat. Could Peter possibly help? Sarah, when she heard, sensing an interesting scenario perhaps, immediately suggested me, and an introduction was arranged at Corks Wine Bar in South Kensington. As Sarah, Peter and I sat waiting with our drinks at the appointed hour, in breezed Tom, resplendent in 1970s twenty-two-inch flares, bomber jacket and sideburns —

rather endearingly behind the times, I thought. I can't say the trousers did anything for me, but he was certainly the best-looking landlord I'd ever seen. I was immediately smitten, but in fact we scarcely succeeded in addressing a remark to each other as Sarah and Peter chattered enthusiastically on without drawing breath. We managed to make a date alone together two nights later in a pub in Kensington Church Street, where we discussed rent and rules, and accordingly agreed that I would be his tenant – a strictly business arrangement, of course. And so it was, for at least five minutes, until I saw his smart little red MG! I was just twenty years old, and in those days many a young girl's heart had fluttered at the sight of a sparkling red sports car – especially when it was driven by a tall, fair Viking-type with warm, laughing blue eyes. Tom drove me home, and as we said goodbye it was natural for me, with my demonstrative ballet background, to kiss him lightly on the cheek. (At least, that's my excuse!) A blush stole instantly over his handsome features, but he didn't look displeased. As I reached the door of my flat, he bent to wave, and nearly reversed into a lamppost before swinging stylishly off into the night. I duly moved into Tom's flat as his tenant, and it was, indeed, the start of the proverbial beautiful friendship.

I was still without a car of my own at this time, and was saving hard for my dream-machine, a little old Morris Minor. I had set my heart on this car, so it was a measure of Tom's charm and persuasiveness that he managed to overturn a lifetime's indoctrination of common-sense and thrift, and convince me that I should spend the money on a skiing holiday in Verbier with him and a group of friends in the spring.

It didn't take his friends long to realise that something more than dedication to the sport was keeping Tom on the nursery slopes rather than on the advanced runs with the rest of them. It was my first attempt at skiing, and Tom, an experienced skier, was an excellent teacher. There's nothing like falling about in a few snowdrifts for bringing a relationship on, and by the end of the holiday we were very much in love.

We had an idyllic romance. It probably sounds very unsophisticated to admit it nowadays, but being with Tom really was such fun, and, in all the friendships I had had with men in the past, I had never known anyone whom I could trust and respect so completely. But I was still taken totally by surprise when there was a knock on my door early in the morning of my twenty-first birthday, and a jubilant Tom asked me to marry him. I knew he had intended to stay up most of the previous night to hear the results of the General Election but I couldn't quite see why the Conservative victory had precipitated such dramatic action. Not that I particularly cared at the time. It was only much later that he admitted he had decided before the Election that he could only propose if Maggie came to power, as only then could he afford to keep me!

I remembered that my mother once told me she kept my father waiting for a week before she gave him her answer, so I felt family pride dictated that I display a degree of restraint, however much I felt like throwing my arms around his neck and shouting, 'Oh yes, yes, yes!' In fact I could only keep him guessing for a day – and I'm sure he wasn't guessing at all. I was absolutely thrilled to be marrying him, though I hadn't been thinking in terms of settling down at all as none of my friends were married. But I suppose you could say I just knew that Tom was the right husband for me, that God had provided him, in a sense. Tom had never come across anything except fairly traditional faith and worship, and although he professed the Christian faith, it wasn't, at that time, very deep-seated. He called himself a 'C of E of the Christmas-and-Easter variety,' but he was open-minded and interested.

Tom is the sort of man mothers-in-law love. He had been, after all, a Marlborough School choir boy. His parents Rodney and Pam lived in a pretty village in Kent from where his father followed the family tradition by managing paper mills in the area. Promoted to head office in London, Rodney spent eighteen months commuting until he felt he had seen quite enough of dawn breaking over Platform One of Swanley station. Going out one fine

May day in 1968 to buy a paddock at auction for his daughter's pony he came home with a hundred acre farm. It changed their lives completely. Night after night, Rodney and Pam sat up reading *Grass and the Dairy Cow*, and eventually they bought a herd. Thereafter 'it was all hands to the plough,' and Tom and his four sisters and any reckless visitors or guests were roped into milking and haymaking. Everyone was judged on their ability to lift a bale of hay. High heels and sophistication were out. Brawn and an appreciation of the smell of silage were in.

Tom had decided he wanted to be a doctor and had chosen his A level subjects accordingly. However a total lack of understanding of physics meant that this career path was thwarted. His father became concerned and made arrangements to see the careers master at Malborough. 'Well, it's either the Army or the Church,' humphed the elderly master with the glass eye, a piece of advice Tom's father, who had driven more than four hours for the interview, felt less than helpful. Tom's new interest in farming, with its lesser emphasis on physics, seemed to offer an alternative. Later on he realised that the rewards from farming a hundred acres were never going to be very exciting and after seeking the advice of a careers analyst completed a course in Estate Management eventually qualifying as a Chartered Surveyor.

The wedding was arranged for October, and the next five months were frantically busy. I had moved out of Tom's flat to share next door with a friend called Sally and began the mountain of preparations that astound every young bride. We took time out, though, for a very important commitment. Tom had been quite involved for some time with a charity called Young Disabled on Holiday, and jointly had arranged to take a party of physically handicapped young people aged sixteen to thirty to France for a week. I very much wanted to go, too. The young people were mostly all in wheelchairs, some badly disabled, others hampered by spasms from diseases like cerebral palsy, and required help from volunteers in a ratio of one to one. Their courage and good humour made a great impact on me. They were on holiday and were determined to enjoy themselves and were not going to let their disabilities get in the way. Very quickly any reservations I had about being with disabled people evaporated. They were quite simply normal people and it was easy to 'see through' their disability. Tom clearly enjoyed these holidays which he found exhausting but very rewarding. Looking back, it was interesting that he should have chosen this particular type of voluntary work. We can only think that God had a hand in leading him in this direction, as nothing could have equipped him so well for the years when his own wife would be confined to a wheelchair. Neither of us knew what lay ahead, but I think without that experience it would have been much more difficult to get through the terrible events to come.

The month before the wedding, I did an intensive Sight and Sound course in typing ('You never know when it might come in useful, dear,' assured my mother, wise as ever). Although I loathe sitting behind a desk, I could see there would be more scope for employment than if I remained simply a dancer. Tom, of course, ever practical, was not blind to the fact that, with the Government's Enterprise Scheme, the forty pounds a week I would earn would be very useful. And I think he hoped for a very convenient secretary in the future!

But the big event for my family, apart from the wedding, was father's ordination. It was clear to all of us how God had led our parents over the years, healing so much of the past, giving them a wisdom and insight, a confidence and faith, that prepared them perfectly for parish ministry. And, again, how remarkable God's planning is, for my father went on not only to have two parishes in north Hertfordshire but to become a part-time chaplain at Addenbrookes Hospital. This post included three neurological units with intensive care.

But disability and pain couldn't have been further from my mind as I walked down the aisle at Knebworth church. My sister Annie, and Tom's two younger sisters Eliza and Rebecca, were my bridesmaids, Richard, my old flatmate with Tom was his best man, and the beautiful church was packed to overflowing with friends and relations. But it was almost as though there was no one else in the building but Tom and I. The worship group sang beautiful choruses and the service was very moving. For me it all passed in a delirious haze of happiness. The reception was held in the old barn at Knebworth House, and then we flew out from England's golden autumn to the sun-drenched shores of St Lucia for a relaxing honeymoon.

I loved being married. Tom was six years older than me, and he built up my confidence and self-esteem enormously. There are pros and cons about getting married young, but perhaps one advantage is that there is a greater flexibility. I hadn't settled into any particular groove (I hope!), and found it relatively easy to adapt to sharing a life with Tom.

I think my mother probably heaved a huge sigh of relief when Tom whisked me off, hoping, I expect, that now I was a married woman I would keep out of the scrapes I had fallen into so many times. In fact, I discovered years later that she had even asked Tom if there had been any serious illness in his family, and had been secretly relieved to hear that they all enjoyed robust good health. The start of our married life boded well, passing happily and uneventfully.

When I finished my typing course in January, the college actually asked me to teach there (an extraordinary proposition, according to my friends, who obviously didn't think of me as the natural office type). Fortunately I was still committed to several dancing jobs with Catherine, so passed that offer by with some relief. Ironically enough, despite all my protestations, later that year I did start a temporary secretarial job at Chelsea College assisting in research on the role of the midwife, and to my surprise I found it fascinating.

Meanwhile my sister Annie was going out with a chap called Giles who had been involved for years in a large and lively Anglican Church in Wimbledon called Emmanuel. Annie had helped in the worship and sung there a few times, and now we got together to work out a worship dance I could do while she sang. That was rather special, being involved in worship with my sister, and I know I was very lucky to have such a good relationship with her. In fact we all got on well. Giles, a lawyer by profession, was warm, kind and fun. He and Tom hit it off well from the beginning – and Tom probably welcomed his moral support when I roped my new husband into ballroom dancing classes that autumn. (Actually, it was a skill he acquired with ease and soon admitted he positively enjoyed.)

Giles and Annie got married in Knebworth in April 1982 and settled down in nearby Clapham, so we saw a lot of them. We were having a good time, but suddenly it all came to an abrupt halt. Christmas was fast approaching, and friends of ours invited us out to a party and a supper of chilli con carne. That night though, Tom and I were so sick we couldn't stand up. At three in the morning, Tom crawled to the phone as I lay groaning on the bathroom floor, and called the doctor. He was not entirely sympathetic, suspecting, I'm sure, that we had simply had too much to drink. However, reluctantly, he agreed to come out, and rather summarily despatched us both with a jab in the bottom to stop us being sick. Despite feeling so awful, I still had the strength to jump a mile when my injection went in as it sent a fierce pain searing right down my leg. Tom, on the other hand, hardly noticed his jab.

For several days we were very unwell, and as we heard from other friends who had been at the party, we realised the problem was food-poisoning, with under-cooked kidney beans the likely culprits. But whereas Tom then began to recover, I was afflicted by another problem. The injection had not only affected my sciatic nerve, but had caused an abscess which gradually grew and grew until it was the size of a golf ball. Red and inflamed, full of pus, the swelling made it impossible to sit down properly while the damage to the sciatic nerve was causing shooting pains down my leg. As ever, I tried to make light of it, but several courses of antibiotics had no effect, and after some weeks I had to go into hospital for an operation to drain the abscess. I then had to go back in for a week's traction to try and free the nerve. Mum came to stay with us for three weeks until I was a bit better, but the nerve trauma rumbled on for nearly nine months, making walking and sleeping difficult.

My family were up in arms about the treatment we had received by the doctor on the first night, as the hospital felt the injection had been carelessly administered. There was an obvious case for legal action, but in the end we let the matter drop. I have always hated confrontation, as Annie pointed out to me at the time, half with amusement, half with irritation. 'You just won't make a fuss, will you, Ju? You'd rather put up with anything than put other people out. Do you remember when we were children and Nigel put that rope around your neck, pretending you were a horse? You were so nearly strangled you began to go blue but you never protested at all!' I laughed and reminded her of when she tried to use my head as a battering ram against a brick wall, and I seemed to think that was fair game too. She was right, but it wasn't that I was simply a masochist or a wimp. It was more that, since the age of three my ballet training had taught me not to show pain, to keep on smiling, that nothing came without effort and suffering – to the extent that by now 'DO NOT MAKE A FUSS' was like the eleventh commandment to me.

Eventually, anyway, the sciatic pain disappeared and the abscess healed, and for a few weeks at least, I felt quite well. Then, suddenly, I was hit by sickness again, but this time I quickly realised there was no cause for alarm. I was simply pregnant. Our first child, Amelia (known from early days as Mimi) was born on August 10th, 1982 to universal delight and thanksgiving after a trouble free pregnancy and delivery.

Tom had been supportive throughout the nine months, coming with me to the antenatal classes, and having a clearer 'birth plan' than ever I did. He was insistent that I shouldn't have any sort of anaesthetic (he had obviously been put right off medical intervention), and during the labour, whilst I would happily have accepted a bullet if they had offered it to me, Tom was politely but firmly refusing all pain relief. Fortunately he provided a certain amount of *comic* relief which perhaps did just as well. Six foot four inches of agitated manhood is not best contained in the confined quarters of a delivery suite. Every time he moved he seemed to crash into the overhead lights or the gas and air machine, and began to resemble John Cleese more and more, until the midwives were in hysterics, and I wondered if they were paying more attention to his antics than to how the delivery was getting on.

I know it sounds a cliché, but I really did find motherhood enjoyable and deeply rewarding. I realised that one of the advantages of having children fairly young was that I wasn't heavily committed to a career. There was no huge salary to forfeit, no status or responsibility to pine for, no dramatic change of environment from office to home. I had enjoyed homemaking so I didn't find the restrictions of feeding and caring for a young baby too oppressive. Besides I had lots of friends and family around for support and was always far too busy to feel isolated or bored.

Tom, too, adored his little daughter, and didn't seem to feel his wings were clipped by the responsibilities of fatherhood. In fact he longed to be able to spend more time at home with the family, but like so many other young husbands was frantically busy trying to make headway in a fiercely competitive job market. He worked long hours often commuting considerable distances. The rat race seemed to be snatching us up and we gradually found ourselves longing for a change. We had moved to a mews flat in Earls Court when we got married, so convenient for us both before Mimi came along. But it's amazing how a baby and all its paraphernalia can make even a sizable place feel cramped. It was becoming increasingly obvious that we needed to move house. Our flat was up two flights of stairs, and it had always been quite an effort hauling shopping and the baby up all these steps. By the time Mimi was a year old, the flat was beginning to feel very cramped as she started to crawl and explore, then when she found her feet and started to toddle about, our search for a new home became urgent.

Living in London had been fun as a single person, but as a parent I really felt that for myself I couldn't bring a child up amid all the fumes with no garden to run around in. So when the estate agents sent us particulars of a double fronted Victorian house in Wimbledon, it sounded ideal, and within minutes I had phoned to make the earliest possible viewing appointment. The property had only just gone on the market and as I walked along the road towards it at nine o'clock in the morning I knew I was the first in the queue of people who would be viewing hourly that day.

I don't go in for dramatic revelations at all, generally, but I must say that as I turned in the gate, I had an almost startling sense of conviction that this was the house for us. Solid and dignified, set in a quiet leafy road with two glorious cherry trees in the front garden, it seemed the perfect place for us, even before I crossed the threshhold and saw all the space and comfort of its bright, attractive interior. As soon as I got home, I telephoned Tom and told him how sure I was that we should buy this house. We knew we had to act fast. We had viewed one in the same road eighteen months earlier and it had been snapped up instantly. Within an hour, I had put in an offer, and by the evening it had been accepted, without Tom even having seen the house!

The quiet confidence I felt that this was God's place for us was borne out by the happiness we experienced throughout our five and a half years there. Wimbledon is full of young families, and with a park right opposite the house I met lots of people with toddlers and quickly made many friends. An old friend Carol who is Mimi's godmother, lived in the same road, and her daughter Fenella was the same age as Mimi, so we were able to exchange children, and help each other out while the girls became staunch friends.

We had already become acquainted with the lively Anglican church of Emmanuel in Wimbledon, through Giles and Annie, and we became very involved during our years there. It had recently acquired a new minister, Jonathan Fletcher, who had a reputation for excellent preaching. The church has an interesting history which has directly affected its character today. Founded in the nineteenth century as a non-denominational fellowship, it was one of the first house churches in the country. As the numbers grew it became evident that a church building rather than a home was needed, and when Emmanuel was established, a clause in the deeds required that it should always be served by an evangelical minister, even though it has never been owned by the Church of England. Because of this, Emmanuel has always been in the charge of an evangelical anglican. It grew steadily, and was particularly lively in the 1920s when it had a very strong missionary emphasis. Then there was something of a lapse until a group of young men working in the City, Giles among them, decided to pour their considerable skills and energies into their local church. Inheriting a godly but somewhat elderly congregation, the young men helped the church to grow steadily so that now in 1991 the electoral roll stands at about 370. Jonathan Fletcher was appointed to take the helm, being a gifted administrator, counsellor and teacher. Young families began to join the church and there are now forty babies under the age of three alone, with dozens more older ones. 'The secret of church growth,' Jonathan told us wisely, 'is to have a good crèche and a good Sunday School!'

As well as the crèche and Sunday School, there was the Mums and Toddlers Group at which I sometimes played the piano and sang nursery rhymes, and a good Wives' Group. Like Holy Trinity, Brompton, it was a church which placed a lot of emphasis on prayer and Bible study, and there was a well-organised structure of fellowship through study groups and prayer triplets — close-knit groups of three committed to prayer and intercession. Tom and I went along to a Bible study at the home of our friends Robin and Sally, and I also became part of a prayer triplet. While I valued the deep friendship and support which grew out of these activities, Tom always kept himself just a little more apart from it all. There's no doubt that women find it easier than men to talk about their faith and share things more deeply, and Tom wasn't the only husband who found our church life rather overpowering and intense.

This situation was of some concern to Jonathan Fletcher at the time, and one or two of the meetings and groups he organised, he admits now, were aimed specifically at drawing the likes of Tom into a deeper Christian commitment. Jonathan believes that 'men are never "at home" at home,' and that some may find it easier to express and explore their faith away from their wives, families and neighbours, in a more male-orientated environment. This explains the success of the lunchtime meetings in the City at St Helen's, Bishopgate, attended now by five to six hundred businessmen. But Tom was not working in the City, so he remained, in his own words, sitting quite comfortably on the fence, fully supportive and interested, but, true to his laid-back, easy going nature, disinclined to become more involved unless the ground moved under his feet. Which it did of course, in due time, shaking his whole world to the foundations and forcing him to reassess his faith – another reason why I have cause to be thankful for the terrible struggles we were soon to go through.

There was considerable interest among the women in the working of the Holy Spirit, and the ways we could use gifts, including music and dance in worship. But although singing new choruses and songs was acceptable to most of the congregation, Jonathan was sensitive to the fact that some of the members might have found dancing a little over the top.

'We wouldn't play rugger in church, would we?!' was his memorable comment, so for the most part we stuck to more traditional forms of worship. The emphasis was on the 'sufficiency of Scripture' as Jonathan put it, that the Word of God didn't need what some might call frills to make it more palatable. Whilst I had to admit that I found dance in worship a powerful visual aid to understanding Scripture, I could appreciate the reservations of others. Besides, what we *were* so fortunate to have at Emmanuel was sound biblical teaching, and I can see now that without the foundation that built I might never have been able to trust God's Word and promises during the times ahead when there was little to hold on to.

Perhaps with an accident record like mine it was courting disaster to go skiing, but a winter skiing holiday in the Alps is almost an institution in Tom's family. We duly set off with little Mimi to spend Christmas 1984 in Thyon, Switzerland with Tom's parents and sister and brother-in-law. Maybe it *was* taking a bit of a risk in one sense as we had just discovered I was expecting our second child, but I didn't intend to do anything reckless and I was becoming a fairly steady skier by now.

The holiday started perfectly. Thyon is a stunning resort and the weather was beautiful. On the second day, Christmas Eve, I set off for a gentle run down the nursery slopes but as I pushed across the hard flat snow my skis suddenly did the splits and I fell heavily forward. My instinctive thought as I crashed down was to protect my stomach and as I tried to throw my weight sideways I jerked my head back sharply and a shooting pain went through my neck. Tom's father sped forward to help me up and as I struggled to my feet we were relieved that no limbs seemed to be broken, but I couldn't move my head without terrible pain. Gingerly we picked our way back across the icy snow to the village and went straight to the doctor who referred us to the resident chiropractor. The medical staff at these resorts are experts in whiplash injuries, and after some agonising manipulation he felt he had managed to get back in two out of three slipped discs in my neck and top back. He put me in a collar, and during the week had six more painful attempts to realign the offending disc, but with no success, so he advised we went to a hospital as soon as we got back to England.

What a blow – and what an idiot I felt. If I had had a spectacular crash speeding down a black run I mightn't have felt so stupid, but to be looking like a victim of a motor pile-up when all I had done was the splits on a flat piece of snow was galling to say the least. I tried to hide the collar with scarves, and celebrated Christmas with as much enthusiasm as I could muster, but the truth was I couldn't move my head, and my neck and shoulders were too sore even to touch. I could feel constant tingling in both hands, and every so often they would be gripped by pins and needles.

On 30th December we arrived back in England and went straight to casualty at St George's, Tooting. A locum said he thought my neck was just bruised and put me in a soft collar, suggesting rest would sort it out eventually. But the pain increased and a week later I went back to casualty. An oriental doctor advised yet more rest, but after another week we had had enough and asked to see a senior doctor who immediately referred us to a consultant rheumatologist. Because I was pregnant, I was unhappy about X-rays, so to a certain extent the specialist was working in the dark, literally! But he put me in a stiff collar and decided we should try physiotherapy. That was dreadful. On the second session, the left side of my neck and my shoulders went into spasm and my hand went numb and after two more sessions, there was a tremendous feeling of compression and I had severe headaches and pain behind my eyes. Traction was the next plan and then hot and cold treatment, but through it all the pain persisted and complications grew.

It was the middle of February and we were getting nowhere. Eventually we decided to make an appointment with a Harley Street specialist, and one dark snowy day mounted the steps of the home of Dr Cyriax, former head of orthopaedic medicine at St Thomas's Hospital. His rooms were like something straight out of a Conan Doyle novel, little changed since the turn of the century, and Dr Cyriax himself, at the age of eighty-two, seemed like a fictional character. He hardly addressed a remark to us but communicated by grunts through an equally elderly nurse who had a barely more extensive vocabulary. But, my goodness, he knew his stuff. He pinpointed almost straight away exactly where the offending disc was and applied some intensive manipulation to my neck. I wouldn't have believed this little man could have been so strong. Even so it took three exhausting sessions over four days before he finally uttered his first words just as I thought my head was about to be wrenched off in his hands. 'Got it,' he exclaimed, followed by a very loud, satisfied grunt, echoed by his nurse. His forehead was beaded with perspiration and I think he was as relieved as we were. It was wonderful to be able to turn my head freely again, instead of feeling as if I had a Frankenstein bolt through my neck. As the weeks passed, the soreness disappeared completely.

The cold damp spring slowly turned into summer. We were expecting another baby in September, so it was all the more wonderful to be mobile again. There were so many people to see, affairs I needed to catch up on. One day, despite a rather nagging headache, I went to Clapham where Annie lived to see a mutual friend of ours. But while I was there, the pain in the back of my head increased until I could hardly move it, and I suddenly realised I was in danger of passing out. I desperately wanted to avoid causing a scene in somebody else's house, but I knew I would never make it back to Wimbledon by myself. So I phoned Annie, trying to make it sound as trivial as possible, to ask if she would run me home. But my voice was a whisper, and by the time she arrived, just minutes later, I could hardly stand. Annie has never been fooled by me, and she bundled me into the back of her car, and drove home to Wimbledon like the wind, scattering cats and old ladies as we roared wildly past, with me huddled and motionless across the back seat.

I wasn't really aware of arriving at home, for the blinding, sickening pain in my head seemed to have clamped every nerve in my body in a vice, and I could barely think or speak. Tom was at work and Mimi was playing with a friend, so Annie called the doctor. When he heard the symptoms, his opinion over the phone was that I had simply caught the nasty 'flu virus which was on the go. 'Stay in bed for three days and dose yourself with plenty of paracetamol and hot drinks,' he advised. But Annie was not to be fobbed off, and she insisted he came out to look at me. When he arrived I vaguely remember bright lights being shone into my eyes. The next moment the doctor was dialling the hospital, and I felt a stab of panic as I heard the words 'suspected meningitis'. Minutes later I was being carried out to an ambulance on a stretcher – just as Tom arrived home from work, a look of bewilderment and apprehension on his face. He stepped almost wordlessly into the ambulance and we sped off to hospital. Vital hours had passed. I was six months pregnant.

The next few days passed in a blur of masks and gowns, injections and drips. I appeared to be in a glass cage which I later discovered was an isolation ward. First they carried out a lumbar puncture and initially suspected bacterial meningitis, and injected me with all sorts of antibiotics. Although I was in such pain I could hardly move my head at all, I tried to resist all these drugs and became very upset. All I could think about was my unborn baby, and I was terrified that the drugs would harm or even kill it. It quickly became apparent that I had viral meningitis, and from then on there was not a lot the hospital could do but let the virus run its course. But we could pray, and I know Annie and my parents phoned dozens of people so that within hours of the illness starting, many were praying throughout the country. For them it was perhaps easier than for my immediate family and friends some of whom found themselves in an alien world of bewildering hospital procedures. No one was allowed to see me without being robed up in protective gowns and masks which made us all feel rather awkward and worried.

I remember Carol coming in and simply tearing off her mask, saying it was all too silly as we had been together only the day before and, anyway, she wasn't in the least afraid of catching anything. Even if this was a rash gesture, looking back, at the time I know I was so touched by her loving act of friendship as I was by the courage and commitment of others who visited – like Jonathan Fletcher who hates hospitals, but came in, only to go home for a stiff gargle afterwards!

I did begin to improve, however, and after eight days in hospital, I was allowed home, very weak and pale.

Although there were weeks of slow recuperation ahead with awful headaches and a painful intolerance to light which meant I had to take things very carefully, my sole thought was for the health of my baby. Scans had not revealed anything wrong with it, but I was small for dates, and we could only wait and see if the vast injection of drugs had harmed it in any way. I never talked about my fears, though, not even to Tom, as I didn't want to burden people with even more worry. But God knew how I felt, and I did find a lot of strength and peace as I shared with Him all my fears.

By September 2nd, though, all my worries were over. Georgie was born, small but perfect, and Tom and I took her home to more than the usual family rejoicing. She developed quite normally, but by now we were learning that health and happiness were not things which could be just taken for granted. Our difficulties had made us all appreciate each other so much more, and had drawn Tom and me together in a deeper reliance on God.

The reality of that faith was tested yet again not long afterwards, when little Georgie herself had a brush with death. At seven months, she caught a flu-type virus and developed a nasty cough. Off her food and sleeping badly, she looked pale and thin. For many days I couldn't go out of the house, but when she seemed to be improving, I asked a friend, Mary, if she would look after her for an hour while I dashed round a supermarket. I pushed Georgie round to Mary's, and, leaving her sleeping peacefully, I set off for the shops. When I returned I was met at the door by a distraught Mary holding Georgie in her arms. In the panic-stricken seconds that followed, I gathered that Georgie had apparently inhaled her vomit while in the playpen, and Mary discovered her, blue and scarcely breathing. The doctor had already been called, and I tried to resuscitate Georgie in the agonisingly long minutes until he arrived. Georgie seemed to be drifting in and out of consciousness, and when the doctor arrived he didn't waste a second. He practically threw Georgie into the back of the car, and drove like the wind to the hospital, crashing red lights and ignoring all speed limits. Without that prompt action, it is doubtful if Georgie would have survived for the hospital discovered that one of her lungs had collapsed and she was being starved of oxygen. For several hours she was a very sick child, never fully regaining consciousness, looking grey and wax-like, until suddenly she opened her big blue eyes wide and smiled at us, her cheeks instantly tinged with a hint of pinkness. What joy and relief flooded through us. Personal pain can be dreadful, but the agony you feel when you think your child is dying is indescribable. From that moment, I resolved to treat every day with my children and husband as a gift, as something so precious, to be infinitely valued. Little did I know that within a few months I would, in effect, be parted from them for nearly three years.

5

Searching For A Diagnosis

'the deadly pestilence that stalks in the darkness . . .'
(Psalm 91: 6)

It all started so innocently, so undramatically. Christmas 1986 was approaching, and our home had never been so full of festivity and excitement. Like all parents, Tom and I were rediscovering Christmas now that we had children of our own. Decorating the Christmas tree recalled all the wonder of that same activity during my childhood, and when Mimi performed a pirouette of delight as we placed the fairy at the top of the tree, I seemed to be watching myself as a little girl once more. Now, as parents, Tom and I were aware of both the privilege and the responsibility of helping our children to discover the real meaning of Christmas beyond the tinsel and turkey.

I lay in the bath one night after this particularly happy family Christmas musing on the wonder of Christ's birth. I had been so deep in thought that I hadn't realised how cold the bath was getting. I jumped up and was just stepping out when there was a crack in my knee like a gun going off — at least, it was so loud that Tom, who was brushing his teeth, jumped and swung round.

'What on earth was that?' he asked.

'I can't imagine, but it came from inside my leg,' I muttered through gritted teeth as I sat on the floor nursing my knee in my hands.

My knee *had* been a little troublesome for the past few

months, clicking loudly whenever I knelt down, but I hadn't paid much attention to it. Who doesn't have a few creaks and cracks as they get older, particularly if they have been a dancer? But this was something more than a harmless click. Not another injury, I thought in disbelief, and tried hard to convince myself that it was probably just a little twist and didn't hurt much at all. I really couldn't bear to ruin the New Year we had planned with my parents so I didn't even let Tom know that I hardly slept that night, and the next day I couldn't put any weight on my knee at all. I almost felt angry with myself for 'cracking up' again, and I would have kicked myself if I could! When Tom saw what a state my knee was in, swollen and inflamed, he insisted we went to casualty to have it looked at.

'I'm sorry, Mrs Sheldon,' the doctor said, shaking his head as he examined my knee, 'but I'm pretty sure it's a torn cartilage. I'll send you along to X-ray just now to check, but I think you will need an operation to remove it as soon as possible.'

'Do we really have to be so drastic?' I asked, appalled at the thought of more hospitalisation. 'If I had some support round the knee, mightn't it knit together by itself?'

It was probably to humour me as much as anything that the doctor did strap my knee, despite the X-rays showing a partial displaced tear of the cartilage, and let me hobble through New Year. I was desperate not to spoil anyone's fun and I tried to hide the bandage and the limp as much as possible – though a pair of crutches are somewhat harder to conceal! I struggled on into the first week of January but then I had to admit the pain was getting worse. An operation was arranged for me straight away at St George's, and I was delighted, if surprised, when the specialist told me I would be able to go home the same day. This was obviously going to be a minor operation, and would cause very little disruption to the family after all.

Tom and I were almost lighthearted as we drove to the hospital early in the morning. It was such a relief to know that in a week or two I would be back to normal. Though there was talk that cartilage removal could result in osteo-arthritis later in life, I felt that was too far away to worry about, and anyway, I reasoned (probably quite wrongly), if I keep fit and active, it's not likely to happen at all. For the moment, the most important thing was that I would be able to get back to being a normal wife and mother again. I never even considered that I might never be able to dance again.

But I wasn't feeling quite so jolly when Tom came to pick me up from the hospital that evening. The operation had been performed under general anaesthetic, and I hadn't realised how dizzy and sick I would feel. Nor had I been prepared for just how sore my knee was going to be.

'You look awful,' Tom observed helpfully, as he came into the room. 'Don't you think it would be sensible to stay the night, and let them keep an eye on you?'

'Not on your life,' I retorted quickly, with as much energy as I could muster. 'If they reckon it's all right to go home now, I would sound really pathetic if I said I couldn't cope. Anyway, it's probably just the heat in here. I'll feel fine, I expect, when I've had a breath of fresh air.'

But a few breaths of air just about finished me off, and I was violently and ignominiously sick in the car park. Poor Tom. He was all for carrying me straight back to the hospital bed, but I was adamant that I wanted to go home, just like an injured animal instinctively returns to its lair to nurse its wounds. I was still sure that a night's sleep would put me well on the road to recovery. In recent years, I had increasingly supported the good-breakfast/brisk walk school of thought (it's said we *do* reveal more and more of our parents' attitudes as we grow older!) and my response to most problems was that there was little that rest, exercise and a bowl of All-Bran wouldn't sort out quite naturally. That was the theory anyway, but there should have been enough instances already in my life, where practicality failed to conform, for me to have been far from optimistic about my present affliction.

Indeed next morning I didn't even feel like eating a good breakfast, let alone taking a brisk walk. My knee was hot and throbbing, and grew even worse if I put my foot to the ground. Of course it was only the first day after the operation and I must expect some discomfort. Stiff upper lip. I was good at that. Lots of practice. As friends drifted in during the day, I was able to convince them, I think, that the whole thing was just a temporary inconvenience, and I would be performing *pliés* in a day or two's time.

Well, I was certainly performing two days later, but it wasn't *pliés*. The pain had got steadily worse, yet I doggedly refused to admit that to anyone, and put up an increasingly desperate act to convince them all that I was really improving. There is an enormous desire to want to please people when you are a patient. Visitors don't want to hear your problems; they just want to be reassured that you are getting better, and I hated to disappoint anyone. In fact, I was to learn slowly and painfully over the next few months and years, that friends who really care for you long to be told the truth, and to be able to share your suffering.

The effort of these visits left me grey and exhausted, though, and Tom was well aware that things weren't too good. Back we went to the orthopaedic specialist who recommended intensive physiotherapy to try and bend my knee which seemed to have locked rigid. After two weeks of fruitless effort with an increasingly frustrated physio, my knee was more painful and just as unyielding. I was relieved when the specialist suggested manipulation under anaesthetic as I was prepared to do anything to get my leg working again and to stop causing a stir about such a trivial matter.

As I came round from the anaesthetic though, rods of hot pain seared through my whole leg. The shock of the pain took my breath away, and I bit my lip and clenched my fists. But more upsetting still, was that the skin on my leg looked strangely discoloured and blotchy, and when I touched it, I might have been jabbing in a thousand tiny needles. When Tom came to pick me up, I was close to tears.

'What's going on, darling?' I asked him, clinging to his

hand. 'The physio doesn't seem to understand why my knee isn't improving, and the doctor has just been muttering something about a malfunction of the sympathetic nerve. But what does that mean?' The tears I had been holding back for days brimmed over, and Tom's kind, open face was clouded and distressed.

'It probably just means the nerves have been irritated by all the interference,' he said comfortingly, but he didn't sound very convincing. 'Let's just give it until tomorrow. I expect we'll see the benefits of the manipulation when the nerves have calmed down a bit.' But I was beginning to dread the nights. There were enough distractions during the day to be able to ignore the pain to a certain extent, and besides I had two little children to care for and a house to run, not the easiest of tasks when you're on crutches. Friends were being marvellous, doing shopping for me and ferrying the girls about, but I wanted to be as independent as possible in the home so that Mimi, in particular, who was just four, wouldn't be more upset than she had to be. In fact, I used to joke about my leg with her and play games of Long John Silver, or make dens with the crutches and an old blanket. But the nights were terrible. After hours of pushing the pain down, pretending it wasn't really there, of keeping up the smile, the full agony of it would engulf me like a wave rushing up a beach, and sleep was only possible in the shortest of fitful snatches as exhaustion overtook me.

As the darkness outside my window began to lighten next morning, I pulled myself up to a sitting position and stared out across the garden and the rows of roof tops to the skeletal forms of the trees on South Park Gardens. The sky was just turning crimson in the east, and an icy February mist clung pinkly around their trunks. If only I could lie on that cold, cold ground, and let the mist curl itself round my body and cool the fire in my leg. When, when will this pain end? God, where are you in all this?

Suddenly a profound feeling of His presence filled the room, and my mind became sharp and clear as a hoar frost. With a flash of illumination, I knew that this pain and disability were going to be with me for some time to come, that some great, extraordinary plan was beginning to unfold in which I had to play my part. Yet somehow I wasn't frightened, for there was an overwhelming sense of God's love and peace flooding over me, and something almost like joy began to well up deep inside. In the half light I reached for my Bible, and it fell open at Revelation. My hands began to tremble as I made out the words:

> Do not fear what you are about to suffer. Behold the devil is about to throw some of you into prison, that you may be tested, and for ten days you will have tribulation. Be faithful unto death, and I will give you the crown of life. (Rev. 2: 10)

For some time I sat still, with tears falling steadily on to the open page. But I wasn't crying because of what I was going to suffer; the thought of pain itself didn't frighten me that much. What touched me far more was this enormous sense of God's love for me, and His care and grace in preparing me for what was to come, giving me a promise and a reassurance which I would be able to hang on to when things got bad. I was so used to having to *earn* praise by achievement and good performance that it was hard to grasp that God was asking me to *do* nothing – except be faithful. He wasn't telling me to fight, to struggle, to overcome, but merely to trust, never to give up hope in Him. I couldn't really imagine what sort of suffering lay ahead, and what was the prison I was going to be thrown in? 'Be faithful unto death . . .' Did that mean I *would* die or just that I would be brought to the brink of death? In an extraordinary way it didn't really matter to me. What *was* important was that God promised me a crown of life not just survival, but victory, joy, a place by His side. It made my heart melt to think He loved me so much to give me this promise. I just prayed that I would be strong enough not to let Him down. Oh Lord, help me to be faithful no matter how hard it gets.

I didn't tell anyone about this experience. Somehow I

felt it was almost too precious, too fragile to share. I didn't want it discussed, analysed, possibly dismissed as a dream. How could I talk about suffering and death with Tom, dear Tom, who was being so loving, positive and encouraging? Besides, maybe the suffering wouldn't last too long; 'for ten days you will have tribulation.' Whilst I knew numbers in the Bible are seldom to be taken literally, ten days didn't seem to symbolise too long a period of time. If the prison was simply going to be pain, perhaps I would be able to hide from everyone just how bad it was.

But within just a few days I was wondering how long I could keep up the cheerful façade. I had never known such unremitting pain, and what was almost worse was the way the skin on my leg couldn't tolerate the slightest touch; my skirt brushing against it, even a breath of wind, felt unbearable. The skin still had a ghastly, mottled appearance, and fluctuated wildly in temperature within minutes. One moment, my leg would feel to me so hot that I thought the skin would blister and pop; the next it would go so cold that I felt as if the flesh itself had frozen like a joint of meat in the freezer. If it was distressing for me, it was equally bewildering for the children who could hardly come near Mummy without her gasping in pain. We had always been a demonstrative, affectionate family, and it upset me deeply that we were having to stop the children running up to me spontaneously to give a hug, or jumping on my lap. Once I couldn't bear it any longer and scooped Georgie up and held her close, tears of pain streaming down my cheeks, while she stretched her little hands tightly round my neck and buried her head, bemused and quiet, in my shoulder.

The doctors, meanwhile, were scratching their heads in perplexity. An uncommon phenomenon, they said, and began to mutter about weird-sounding conditions called Algodystrophy, or Sudeck's Atrophy. The books described it as a clinical syndrome characterised by pain, dystrophic tissue changes, and local disturbance of the autonomic function in a limb. But no one seemed to know quite how to treat the problem. We struggled on for a few more weeks, Tom getting more and more exhausted from getting both the girls up, dressed and breakfasted before dashing off to his work, whilst I staggered about trying to tidy the house, do the ironing, cook meals. By the middle of February, despite the fact that we couldn't really afford it, we had had to advertise for a mother's help, and were fortunate to find a lovely, caring girl from Kent called Claire who wanted a temporary job until she went to college in the autumn. As we were to discover, nannies can be a very mixed blessing, but Claire fitted in very easily and was a great help. We were so reliant on other people, and friends and family couldn't have been more supportive and helpful. Jonathan Fletcher visited regularly to encourage and pray with me. Sally, Claire, Carol, Julia, Pat, Susie, and so many others, were all angels of mercy, doing shopping for me, having the children to play, even cooking meals for us.

My helplessness drew me closer to people than I would ever have been in full health, and there grew a depth to one or two of my friendships that I gradually recognised as something rare and very precious. Seldom in adult life do we allow others to see our weaknesses and faults; we try to present a strong, positive, attractive image to the world, and the busyness of our lives leaves us with little time or opportunity for sharing our deeper thoughts or fears. But times of crisis cut through all the superficiality and give a new urgency to openness and honesty; pride or reserve have to bow to the demands of survival. Not with everyone, I suppose. Years of habit still produced the automatic, 'Fine, thanks!' to the enquiry about my health from people I didn't know well. But where deep trust and commitment were growing I slowly began to see that here was a platform of safety where I could share the pain and the fear.

For a long time, though, I did find it incredibly difficult not to just switch on the smile all the time and insist I could cope. Most people withdrew at that point, some with their eyes clouded and troubled, sensing a barrier, but others quite happy to take it at face value, relieved, perhaps, not to get more involved. It's common, after all, for people to feel awkward and embarrassed when faced with illness or disability. But there was one person, in particular, whose love and encouragement were more instrumental than any others in bringing me through that time. Penny, who had sung with Cloud, had married Rupert, a merchant banker, and come to live just ten minutes' walk away from us in Wimbledon. For a while they were involved with Emmanuel Church with Penny and I getting together to sing and on one occasion lead worship in the church. We both belonged to the Wives' Group at Julia's, and had prayed together a few times, but I didn't know at the time that for some months, even before my illness, Penny had felt God saying she would be very involved with me in some way. So as the condition in my leg deteriorated, Penny poured all her strength and faith into me, visiting every day, the whole time pointing me to God's love and care for me. We didn't, at that time, know what a long and terrible journey lay ahead, but even if we had, I know her commitment and self-sacrifice would have been just as great. I felt Penny was never fooled by my attempts to conceal the pain. So often her clear blue eyes would give me a piercing look and then fill with compassion and sorrow as she saw the real truth behind the act. Not that she ever spoke anything negative to me. She always believed that God would heal me and constantly spoke of His power and faithfulness.

Since the doctors felt at a loss how to cure the condition, the next best thing was to try and alleviate the symptoms, so it was decided I should go into St George's for nerve blocks to stop the pain. Although these blocks would only give relief from pain for hours or at the most a day or two I think it was hoped that by breaking into the cycle of nerve malfunction, it would trip the nerve into normal response just as suddenly as it had slipped out. Twice a week, seventeen visits in all, somebody had to drive me to the day ward for a Guanethedin nerve block. Because the nerves that control the blood flow and circulation were affected, the veins in my leg were almost impossible to find, so my visits would begin with me sitting with my foot immersed in a bowl of hot water to raise the veins for the needle.

The first few times, I had a companion in the next bed. He had fallen through a plate glass window a few years before, and still suffered awful pain from the nerve damage. As he was a keen darts player and enjoyed a pint or two, he told me the pain severely restricted his pastimes! I learnt a lot about darts as we waited for the anaesthetist, and we buoyed each other up with jokes, and discussed which beers were best (though the sum total of my ability in this area was to be able, just, to tell draught from bottled). We would tease each other about who would be first, but as his block was into the arm it was a bit quicker, and he was usually trundled off first. Somehow seeing him go through it always made me feel a little more brave. By the time it was my turn, my neighbour's curtains would be drawn back again, and as he lay quietly he would offer, 'It's not that bad, Julie,' looking pale and still. I knew he was being kind.

Then the laborious search for a suitable vein would begin. Eight times was quite usual to have the 'butterfly' needle inserted into non-existent veins. The doctor would become irritated, and the nurse edgy for it was her job to hold tightly round my calf to help raise the vein. Meanwhile I would be gritting my teeth and praying that 'this time' would be the one and I would hear the comforting words, 'We're there!' This ritual became very distressing. It really is very painful having a needle inserted anywhere in your foot and I remember once imagining how terrible it must have been for Jesus having *nails* banged into his feet. Desolation, fear and pain swept over me as the needle was jabbed in repeatedly. I tried to pray for the doctor and nurse, but sometimes all I could hear in my mind was, 'My God, why hast thou forsaken me?'

Once the needle was in a satisfactory position, a tourniquet was wrapped very tightly around the top of my thigh, secured and bound with sticky bandage. The tourniquet was the same as the black cuff used on your arm for taking blood pressure, and this would be pumped up until the blood flow into my leg was temporarily stopped. Then the anaesthetist would inject the nerve block into the awaiting vein in my foot. It would be a diluted mixture, but still the burning, searing pain would envelop my whole being. Then my leg would be supported above my body by the nurse for at least fifteen minutes to allow the block to attach itself to the offending nerves around my knee. Afterwards I would be wheeled back to the ward and left to lie still next to my companion until we felt able to go home.

The procedure was difficult and, like any treatment involving anaesthesia, carried an element of risk. On one occasion, the pressure inside the inflated cuff caused it to explode just after the drug had been administered. Like a dam bursting, the drug flooded through my body and into my brain. Terror gripped me as I felt myself drowning under the wave, and the doctor and nurse began to fly around the room. All I could hear were rapid, resounding thuds and then came more fear as I realised they were my heart beats. I suppose the doctor must have given me some sort of antidote as gradually the turmoil inside me subsided, but I felt very unwell for several hours. It was hard to convey to Tom what had happened and the hospital staff didn't mention that anything had gone wrong so I felt very isolated in my fear as I faced the next block alone three days later.

I couldn't have carried on with this bizarre form of torture if it hadn't been for the immense benefits. Although the treatment couldn't cure the condition it gave me blissful relief from the pain, sometimes several hours completely free of discomfort in which I could rest and regroup before the next onslaught. Once or twice, though, the block had no effect at all, and then the wait until the next one seemed like an eternity.

After about ten blocks I began having them in the Oncology Unit for cancer patients which was next to the day ward. A Sister called Jane had been so kind and smiling every time I hobbled past on my crutches, and once she had asked me in for a cup of coffee and a chat. The Unit had about four beds and a couple of comfy 'real' armchairs, not hospital ones. There was a little kitchen corner where patients could make their own tea and coffee, a fridge full of cold drinks, and an atmosphere of calm and peace. I watched many people come into that Unit to receive their chemotherapy, with thin drawn faces and bald heads, but each face would light up as Jane welcomed them in and made them completely at home with her warmth and thoughtfulness. Any fear or misunderstanding I might have had about chemotherapy dissolved in that happy little room. There was so much suffering represented there, but Jane's love for each of her patients seemed to make it bearable for them. I was beginning to see already how that little extra care, time and patience can make all the difference to those requiring hospital treatment. I was to experience both the best and the worst of nursing care in the months to come.

Although the nerve blocks should ultimately improve a condition, as with chemotherapy, the treatment itself can make a patient very sick and exhausted. For me, each visit also required a great effort of will to surrender myself voluntarily to more pain, so by the time the course was finished, I was mentally very low. It so happened that Tom, whose greatest passion is sailing, was due to compete in a sailing championship the weekend the treatment was completed. Claire was due to leave just prior to this, and a new nanny was starting straight away, so in the couple of weeks beforehand I had urged Tom to go, keen to show how much better my leg was getting, and that I could cope without him for a few days. But when the weekend came, I had had five days of a nanny who was turning out to be a walking disaster, the children were unsettled and difficult, and although I tried to wave Tom off cheerfully, all my strength and courage seemed to evaporate as the front door closed. Suddenly I felt so vulnerable, so alone. I realised immediately how much I had relied on his comfort and help in the evenings.

For the first time ever, I phoned up Penny one evening, and with tears burning my cheeks told her I couldn't cope any longer. Penny didn't waste time talking on the tele-

Above: 1960: early days at the barre.

Below: Julie with brothers Nigel and Alec, and sister Annie.

Above: Nine-year-old Julie with Peek-a-Boo at a horse show.

Below: Budding ballerinas Annie and Julie.

Top: The Elmhurst
Summer Show. Julie,
right, with other
Elmhurst Ballet School
students.

Above: Posing by the
pond at Elmhurst!

Right: Pride comes
before a fall. Skiing in
Switzerland shortly
before the neck injury.

Above: Tom and Julie after their engagement in 1979.

Below: Julie's parents, David and Jean Mumford.

Left: "Two's Company": Julie and Catherine in a "Superman" promotion for Warner Bros, 1979.

Below: From "Superman" to "Superdrug": "Two's Company" in the National Hospital, 1989.

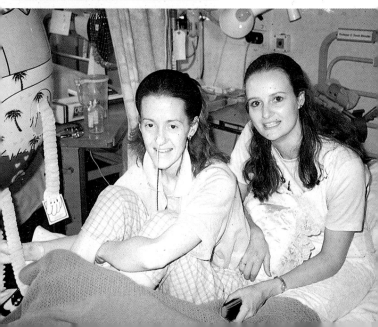

Left and Above: Allowed home from hospital for a weekend.

Below: An outing with Mimi and Georgie to Kew Gardens.

Left: A reunion with Canon Jim Glennon – having last seen Julie in intensive care, he did not recognise her.

Above: May 5th 1990: "In the Pink" party celebrating Julie's recovery.

Below: Nigel, Annie, Julie and Alec "In the Pink".

March 1991: Mimi, Julie, Tom, Georgie and Rosie the dog.

phone. Within minutes she was at the house, her face contorted in an agony of failure that she hadn't been able to avert this, for apparently she had always feared that my refusing help might eventually lead to some sort of crisis. I didn't expect her to say anything. There weren't, after all, any answers. I just needed to know I wasn't alone. All we could do was pray together. And as we did so I had an amazing experience.

I suddenly saw in my mind a picture of a plate and on it was a ballerina in full classical costume dancing gracefully. She was smiling but somehow I could tell that underneath she was crying. In a split second I knew that God was asking me to offer up to Him all those years of ballet training, all that hard, unrelenting discipline which had taught me never to show my feelings, which had set such store on performance and achievement. It seemed, as I watched, that God was also wanting me to surrender all the hurts and disappointments of my life, particularly the time I was dropped and broke my back. As I shared the vision with Penny, she helped me to pray it through, but we were both aware that there were depths of emotion there which might take a long time to draw out.

Certainly as soon as I got over my 'lapse', I was back, next morning, to business as usual in my attempts to please everyone I saw with a positive impression of my condition. Soon I didn't have to pretend things were improving. The pain lessened, and I was nearly able to tolerate touch on my skin. I could put weight on my leg and even managed to walk short distances without crutches. It was midsummer and everyone was in a wonderful mood now that there were clear signs of improvement. Friends and family breathed a huge sigh of relief, and the doctors became hopeful of a full recovery. I was so glad to be able to greet people with good news, and, most of all, to be a slightly more normal wife and mother.

Our second nanny, an extremely large girl given to eating vast quantities of junk food and secret midnight raids on the larder, left us after eight weeks, to our immense relief. In Tom's view she was so vague as to be unsafe with the children. We hoped we would try never to have live in help again, and fortunately I was improving so much that I thought I could cope fine on my own. By October I was so much better that Tom and I felt we could slip off for a short holiday in Majorca as a sort of celebration for the end of ten very trying months without any time for one another. True I was conscious of a new niggling pain in my hip, but we just put it down to uneven walking and general muscle wastage. Far more important was the fact that I could stroll gently round the sights arm in arm with my husband, walk down to the beach and back, and swim in the beautiful warm water.

As I lay in the sun and watched Tom floating idly on his back in the sparkling sea, I felt that at last we were just like any other ordinary couple on holiday. I was sure that now we would be able to build our lives together, provide a sense of security and stability for the children whose short lives had been so disrupted. I thought of home, and Mimi who had just started school. She was finding the new experience a trying one, having spent so much of the last two years being farmed out to other people. It upset me deeply to see her obvious anxiety and insecurity when there was any new change or challenge in her life. I was desperately keen to establish a steady, quiet routine for the girls, and for them to know that from now on I was going to be the one looking after them at home. Mimi had often displayed an aura of gravity and sadness which suggested a sense of responsibility far beyond her five years, and I longed to restore her to the attitude of carefree fun and happiness she should be feeling at her age.

It was a devastating blow to me then, soon after getting back to England, to have to admit to myself that the pain was getting worse again. A lot worse. I couldn't bear to disappoint everyone, to cast shadows over all their happiness, so for several weeks I tried again to hide it. As usual it was Penny who saw through my act, and tried, gently, to get me to share what was going on inside – not just the physical pain but the equally distressing mental anguish of fear, bewilderment, even anger. I think I would still have resisted letting her know how I was really feeling for a lot longer if it hadn't been for a very special experience she had just gone through which, for her, put a whole new perspective on my illness.

'It happened last week, Julie, when I was listening to John Irvine's sermon at church,' she explained carefully. 'I had been so upset and worried about you, but, most of all, I felt so frustrated that no one really knew what the matter was with you, or realised how bad it was. Even if you don't talk much about the pain, I can see what it's like, and I've felt so helpless. Well, as John Irvine was talking, I kept seeing you in my mind, all grey and drawn, trying to smile but crying inside, and suddenly I heard him reading the verse from 2 Timothy 1: "I know whom I have believed, and am convinced that He is able to guard what I have entrusted to Him for that day."

'It was as if God was speaking to nobody else in the church but me, and I just knew that He was telling me that I needed to trust Him with your illness and healing, that even though I should pray and pray, and never give up hope, you were not my burden and responsibility. It sort of set me free, because the worry and pain of seeing you suffer was almost stopping me from giving you the strength and support God wants me to bring. So I just want you to know,' she finished, almost shyly, her eyes shining with tears, 'that you can tell me exactly what you're going through, no matter how bad or awful it is, without feeling that you're burdening me or being a failure. Because God's never going to give up on you, and nor am I!'

I have almost never cried in front of anyone, but I did then. This was the same sort of acceptance, of wonderful, unconditional love I had glimpsed that early morning when God had given me His promise from Revelation. I was loved even though I was weak; I was of worth even though I could achieve nothing; I was cared for even when I could give so little. It seemed God was using this illness to bring to the surface things which needed healing almost more than my body. Perhaps, as Penny was privately realising, I *couldn't* receive His healing until these problems had been sorted out. And that meant a painful process of breaking down years of resistance to showing weakness or need. So began a series of extraordinary and wonderful interventions by God to reveal His greater plan for my life.

Right from the beginning Penny had known that she had a part to play in my situation. She says it was never a duty or a bind to visit or pray for me. It seemed her natural role to support me and though at times my condition must have been very frustrating for her she seemed to have an assurance that eventually all would be well. In her concern for me she phoned a gifted counsellor at HTB to plead for help – and was apparently very taken aback when the woman replied briskly, 'If Julie wants me, she'll ring me.'

But as she sat and thought it over she realised that she was trying to push God to act in her time and way, and that perhaps this particular moment or method were not His will. As she tried to come to terms with that, she seemed to hear God speaking to her, saying, 'Do the works I set in front of you. Be obedient to my promptings.' And feeling humbled but grateful, she prayed God would just make those promptings abundantly clear.

Within a day or two of that experience, Penny heard that Joyce Huggett was speaking at HTB and strongly felt that I should go and hear her. Joyce Huggett has a wealth of experience in counselling and is the author of several Christian books. It was a major operation getting me into London and finding a suitable space in a packed church hall for me and my crutches. By the time we were installed, I was almost fainting with pain. But I forced my mind to concentrate on what Joyce Huggett was saying and found myself engrossed in her message of 'Listening to God' and learning how to come into His presence. Then there followed a time of worship. Unknown to me, Penny, beside me, was shaking all over in anticipation of some great breakthrough (or breakdown!) in me, so strong was her sense that God had brought me there for a purpose, but I just had my eyes shut and felt wonderfully calm and peaceful in an atmosphere of sensitive worship. Then, just as the service was drawing to a close, a woman stepped up to me quietly and knocked me for six with her words.

'Hello. My name is Virginia, and before I came to the meeting today the Lord told me I would meet a girl called Julie with long fairish hair and that God wanted to encourage her.'

The tears in her large brown eyes matched the ones springing up in my own. My crutches were hidden out of sight under the chair and I was sitting down. There was no outward sign that I was disabled and there were plenty of other girls with long fair hair. I was completely bowled over by this sign of God's care for me and for a moment I couldn't speak. But even as I struggled to find the words to thank her and question her further, Virginia had squeezed my hand and disappeared into the crowd of people milling in the aisles.

This word of encouragement came at exactly the right time and in just the right way for me – and for Tom. He had not had any experience of gifts of the Spirit such as visions and prophecy, and, being a down-to-earth, practical sort of chap would probably have been rather wary of anything too dramatic or way out. But this simple episode was remarkable enough for us to realise God was at work without Tom being put off. And as November turned into December, we desperately needed that reassurance. The pain in my hip was excruciating. Diagnosed first as bursitis or inflammation of the hip, the condition was now being called migratory Algodystrophy. This uncertainty about the cause of my problem was one of the most difficult aspects of those weeks, for, inevitably, there arose the question in some people's minds that the whole thing might simply be psychosomatic. Of course my family and close friends who knew me well never for a moment considered that the pain was a symptom of hysteria or depression. But for the doctors, who at that time could find no organic cause for the condition, this suggestion presented itself with growing plausibility, and as my treatment progressed, it became clear to us that this was fundamentally the way they viewed my case.

This attitude hurt me very deeply, the more so as it came after another remarkable experience, this time at the London Healing Mission, which I had been told about by Virginia, the woman who came up to me at HTB. This organisation is run by Andy and Audrey Arbuthnot as a centre of Christian renewal, counselling, and healing. Over twenty people work together at the Mission as a spiritual family, with seven hundred more affiliated as prayer intercessors. Prayer, counselling and ministry are provided by appointment, and on Thursdays two services of worship, communion, thanksgiving and intercession are held in the chapel. Seventy to ninety people come to each service, with a variety of needs, physical, mental, spiritual, marital. Andy Arbuthnott, an ex-merchant banker now ordained, usually preached, and many received ministry for their pain, shock, stress or worry. Each member of the team at the London Healing Mission has their particular gift or role, but the hallmark over all their dealings with people is love.

As the pain in my hip and leg increased, I phoned Virginia for I somehow felt that God was wanting to use her to help me in some way. Virginia suggested I came along to a service, so I asked Penny if she would take me there. Walking even with crutches was now almost impossible, so it took a tremendous effort to reach the Mission, struggling to get in and out of the car, up the steps and through doors in bitter December weather. But as Andy preached I knew I was meant to be there. His talk was about Job, in particular from chapter three where Job, amidst all his suffering and afflictions, cries: 'What I feared has come upon me; What I dreaded has happened to me'. (Job 3: 25).

Andy's message was about the power of words to act almost like a curse – or a blessing – upon us. The negative effect can be to produce a foothold of fear in our minds which could allow, he suggested, Satan to bring about the very thing we wanted most to avoid. Suddenly, a light seemed to be thrown upon all that was happening to me. In a flash, I saw myself as a little girl with glandular fever being told by the doctor that I wouldn't be well for a year, and, indeed, the illness dragged on and on. Then I remembered the warning of the orthopaedic surgeon when I was twelve that I would be in a wheelchair by the age of thirty if I continued to dance, and the similar grim forecast of the specialist when I broke my back – and here I was, helpless and disabled. Last of all I recalled my own bitter exclamation after I missed my second demonstration at the Lyceum with Madam Espinosa. I could see how I had been living under a shadow of calamity most of my life, and although I had always been fighting all obstacles and threats with my conscious mind, perhaps, deep down, seeds of fear and dread *had* grown up insidiously to wreak a harvest of destruction.

Only God truly knew what the reality was, but at the call for ministry I went forward and allowed one of the counsellors to anoint me with oil. As she did so, she took authority over all powers of darkness that might be coming against me, and broke the chains of those 'prison sentences' which I had received.

I sat quietly with my palms upwards. I felt an immediate release of some inner heaviness and a whole weight of fear left me. I surrendered to God all those bitter memories, and felt a sort of healing oil of His Spirit flowing through my mind, soothing all the hurt. It didn't even occur to me at the time that there was no prayer for physical healing. This inner turmoil seemed to be at the root of much of my sickness, and I was left with an overwhelming sense that as God brought this mental and spiritual healing to completion, so my body would be made whole too. Penny's eyes shone with joy as she drove me home that night, for she, too, felt an absolute confidence now that as God freed me, so I would be healed physically. The door had been broken open during that service, and now it was up to me to overcome years of habit and fear, and walk out of my prison.

It amazes me that so often when God does something very powerful in our lives there is often a savage evil counter-attack. So, looking back I suppose it wasn't surprising that within just two weeks of going to the London Healing Mission, I was back in hospital, this time in a hospital in Wimbledon following a marked physical deterioration. Christmas was just a week away and this new setback was a blow for the whole family, the more so as nobody knew even then what the nature of the illness really was. Algodystrophy was now beginning to seem an inadequate diagnosis for the extreme pain and increasing disability. I could now barely sit up. At the hospital all they could do was give me morphine injections every few hours to control the pain, but even so it was often like a dreadful nightmare. Cortisone injections into my knee and hip were given, but the pain still grew worse. Things looked very bleak.

The thought of being away from the family at Christmas was breaking my heart, so I was overjoyed when the hospital said I could go home for Christmas Day – with a doggy-bag of drugs to help me through! Mimi and Georgie were wildly excited, so ready to believe that everything was all right again because Mummy was home, whilst between Tom and me there was a special closeness and tenderness. The future seemed so uncertain, and we wished the day could go on for ever. It was grim indeed to return to my hospital room which seemed so cheerless despite the valiant efforts by staff and friends to decorate it festively.

New Year's Eve came, a day I had been dreading for many reasons, not least of which was the fact that Tom had to leave me later that day to take the children down to Kent to stay with his parents for a couple of days. In the afternoon Penny and Rupert had come in to see me and Tom arrived with a bottle of champagne. We all tried desperately to be jolly and enthusiastic as we toasted each other with sparkling glasses, but there was a hollowness about our laughter and once or twice a silence fell. New Year's Eve can be an emotional day, a time for looking back over the year's joys and tribulations, and of facing the year ahead with fresh hope and determination. We were all still clinging to what we felt God had promised concerning my healing, but the reality we could see with our eyes was not an encouraging one. The time came for Tom to leave and I couldn't speak. For a moment I held him tight and then he was gone.

It was as if some buffer against the pain was taken away. As before, the full force of it swept over me and instinctively I reached out to Penny and Rupert. Instantly they took my hands, praying quietly but strongly, and then suddenly, through the agony in my mind, I heard Rupert's voice speaking, loudly and steadily – except there was an authority and power about it which made me realise this was a prophecy, a word from God Himself:

My child, I am well pleased with you. I delight in you and love you greatly. I think of you all the time. I have cried when you have cried, and I have suffered as you have suffered. Have faith and trust in me, for I am with you always. Put your hand in mine and walk with me along the path that I have prepared for you. Endure but for a short while, my little one, and you will share with me my crown of glory, and partake of the great and wonderful joys that I have prepared for you.

We were all filled with awe. Here was the same message of encouragement He had given me at the beginning, though still nobody knew about that. For Penny and Rupert, the word was a reminder that God is always in control, sovereign over all our circumstances. He may allow suffering, so that He can do a greater work within us and through us, drawing us, in His time, into a deeper experience of His love and blessings.

Penny continued coming in to see me every day and kept me hanging on to God's promise. Annie and Giles, too, visited regularly and tried to keep me cheerful. I certainly felt as if I was in the Pit, but I wouldn't give up. I was conscious too of my old 'don't-make-a-fuss' attitude from my ballet days, and indeed, in hospital you are constantly exhorted to 'be good' in just that way: 'Be a good girl and use the bed pan,' 'Be a good girl and don't complain about the pain.' It was my old battleground of perform, perform,

perform, and I found I was being forced against my will back on to the desperate treadmill of trying to please.

But what made it far worse was that gradually I sensed the attitude of the doctors and nurses hardening. At first I had merely been a disappointment and a puzzle in my failure to respond to their treatment. But now their suspicions that it was all in the mind grew, for some of them, into a conviction. The nurses became more brittle and cool towards me until eventually one of them rounded on me, hands on hips, and exclaimed, 'Why don't you go home and look after your children? Don't you love them? You lie there on your back with everyone running round you. Why don't you get up and start being a proper wife and mother?'

Whether this was meant to be shock tactics, I don't know, but it devastated me. The greatest torture to me was that I couldn't care for my family properly, that I couldn't even hold my little girls who came in almost every day with the same question, 'When are you coming home, Mummy?' Penny came in that afternoon and found me sobbing bitterly. When she heard what had happened, she prayed for me, and as she did so had a picture of God wrapping me round with a cloak, a cloak which would protect me from all words spoken. I felt a sense of peace, despite everything, and that shield was to help me through the storms of the next three weeks.

The orthopaedic specialist who had been treating me now had to admit he was completely stumped, so he called in a physician friend of his. From the start it was evident he, too, thought privately that the problem was psychosomatic, and he was determined to get me out of bed. Intensive physiotherapy and walking were decided to be the answer, and even though I could hardly sit up without help, I was determined not to be labelled depressive or non-cooperative.

When the physio came to my room, I summoned every ounce of strength and levered myself into a sitting position on the side of the bed. With my arm over the physio's shoulder, I tried to walk across the room, pain hitting me like rounds of machine gun fire until I began to shiver and shake. But I refused to give up. Day after day I half-walked, half-crawled down the corridor, clinging on to the rail that ran along the wall. Often I would collapse and the physio had to drag me back to my feet, all the time asking for 'just a bit more effort'. Sometimes I simply couldn't get up again, and a porter would have to carry me back to bed. 'Got the vapours again, 'ave we?' he would ask cheerfully. Perhaps he just meant to be kind, but there always seemed to be the suggestion that I was putting it all on, attention-seeking, I suppose. Afterwards they would leave me alone for hours, and my body, aggravated by the stress of movement, would be in agony. It was like being burnt at the stake, tongues of pain licking round my limbs, consuming more and more of me with an insatiable hunger. Sleep was impossible.

It was a dark time. There was one day which Penny calls Black Wednesday of which, quite honestly, I remember little, but apparently she came in to see me and found me completely out of control with pain, unable to respond to her desperate attempts to communicate. Rushing off to find a doctor, Penny was absolutely staggered when he refused even to come and see me. Penny dashed back to my room and met Tom coming out white-faced and upset. Penny clung to him and for a few minutes she cried on Tom's shoulder. They stood holding my hand, praying until I stopped thrashing about and either fainted or fell into a sort of sleep. When I awoke some time later all I could remember was having a dream of my family and friends gathered in a circle around Jesus, with me kneeling at His feet. But instead of worshipping Him, I was pleading, 'Please show me your face, I can't see your face.' I felt desolate.

The new doctor who was treating me was not impressed by my progress. Despite all my efforts, I was becoming more and more immobile, and although I didn't dare tell him or the nurses the injections seemed no longer to make any difference. Then, a few days later, the doctor confided in Tom that they were giving me placebos, and, since I wasn't complaining of more pain, they were probably right in assuming my condition was psychologically induced. How Tom didn't hit him, I don't know, but when Tom told me I was furious and would have impaled him with my crutches if I could. It brought back to me so vividly the awful time at the Royal Ballet when the doctors told me I hadn't really broken my back, and I was so angry I refused all medication for nearly two days until I was barely conscious. Tom asked to see a pain specialist, but his attitude seemed much the same. 'You must understand, of course, Mr Sheldon, that we're all in some degreee of pain the whole time, if you stop and think about it. The crucial thing is our consciousness of, and response to, that pain. Our pain threshold. Mrs Sheldon's is obviously quite low.' How can you reply to that sort of comment? We felt hopeless. Again, it was dear Penny who prayed this through with me, banishing that lie, and seeing a picture of three angels coming to stand guard round my bed, with Jesus watching from the chair next to me, checking the drugs and the people who came in.

But the crunch came the following week when the doctor came and sat on my bed. He was quiet for a moment, staring at his hands, but when he looked up I was shocked by his face. It was white with anger.

'This can't go on, Mrs Sheldon,' he snapped, trying to keep his voice low. 'You'll just have to pull yourself together. There's nothing the matter with you so far as we can see, and the sooner you admit it's all in the mind, the quicker you'll get better and save everyone a lot of time and trouble. You've GOT to get out of this bed and start walking. Think of your family. They need you at home, not lying here like an invalid being selfish.'

He was almost shouting now, on his feet and pacing up and down the room. Part of me felt a detached sense of pity at this man's obvious frustration and irritation, at the arrogance of the medical expert's inability to admit he is defeated by a situation. But by far my overwhelming feeling was sheer fury. I was too angry even to reply, and deeply, deeply hurt too, that after all my efforts I was being condemned. I refused to let him see me cry in case he labelled that as more hysteria, and I turned my face to the wall. A minute later, the doctor marched out, slamming the door.

When Tom arrived that evening I was at the end of the line. We had to get out of that hospital and I was all for going straight home that night, but we both knew in our hearts that I couldn't possibly cope at home. Where could we go? Whom could we ask for a second opinion?

By one of those extraordinary 'coincidences', we discovered within the next day or two that the new boyfriend of Tom's youngest sister, Bec, was the son of one of the world's top neurologists. Professor Marsden was based at the National Hospital for Nervous Diseases, Queen's Square, and Andrew, his son, offered to speak to his father about us. Professor Marsden was happy to discuss the matter, so Tom phoned him up, and to our relief he agreed to arrange to transfer me to the National Hospital for tests. At last we seemed to be getting somewhere.

Penny and Rupert had been preparing for a house move for weeks and the thought of separation was heartbreaking for us all. Penny, in particular, felt very flat and depressed. She had been emotionally involved with us for such a long time. As she walked with Rupert through Richmond Park on a Sunday afternoon in late January, through dripping, leafless trees, she poured out how raw and stripped bare she felt, as if all her emotions were exposed like nerve endings. Then as they neared the road, an ambulance flashed past, and to their utter amazement through the rear window they saw the back of Tom's fair head. They had not been aware that I was being transferred to the National Hospital that day, and as the ambulance disappeared round the corner, Penny felt a great release of responsibility as if God was lifting us out of her hands, and showing her that we were in His care. 'Lord, they're yours,' she whispered. They moved to Tunbridge Wells soon afterwards, and Tom and I began the next stage of our battle for life alone.

6

Dystonia Confirmed

'. . . and the plague that destroys at midday'
(Psalm 91: 6)

Every jolt and swing in the ambulance was excruciating, and I clung on to Tom's hand. Laboriously we made our way along the crowded roads, past the British Museum, and finally into the quiet square which housed the London Homeopathic Hospital and the National Hospital. As the ambulancemen carried me out on the stretcher, I caught a glimpse of the tall, dignified Victorian façade. It seemed to speak of authority, dependability, and I felt a surge of hope. We now had the best chance in the world of finding out what the problem was.

I was taken up several storeys in a cramped, rickety lift, and put in a side ward with five beds. An enormous window stretched right across one wall, and the room was stark, but bright and spacious. Nevertheless it felt strange coming from the security and quiet of a private room into the bustle of an open ward, and I had lost so much confidence in the hospital at Wimbledon that I now felt vulnerable and insecure. My eye was caught by the green print on the pillowcases: 'The National Hospital for *Nervous Diseases*.' Panic filled me. Was I in a psychiatric hospital? As Tom left, the tears fell. A deep well of mental pain seemed to have been tapped, and I just couldn't stop the sobs as huge waves of pent-up feelings burst over me. It was then I discovered how very special the nurses at the

National Hospital are. I was expecting to be told to pull myself together, but instead a gentle nurse called Imelda came and sat on my bed and just held me. At first she didn't even say anything, but just stroked my hair and rocked me gently. It was a long time before the tears stopped, but when I started to breathe more easily she softly coaxed me into talking about what was upsetting me. It was some days before I felt confident enough to be able to talk a little about how I felt, but all the nurses were so loving and caring that the atmosphere of acceptance and understanding healed a lot of the mental scars of the past few weeks. Many of the nurses seemed to be Irish, and it was medicine in itself to hear their soft, lilting voices, ready laughter and down-to-earth good sense. Their faith was obviously very important to them as well, and you somehow felt the Lord's compassion and tenderness in all their actions. Angels of mercy, I suppose they seemed to all of us who lay suffering or helpless in bed.

We were a diverse and motley crew. At first my instinct was to remain completely distant and private. It takes quite a mental and physical effort to establish a relationship with other patients when you are bed-bound and have to shout across the room. But we were all joined by the common bond of a difficult neurological disorder, like Multiple Sclerosis and Parkinson's disease. Eventually the need for human contact and support drew most of us out. Some barriers were greater than others, and I have to confess I had a lot of problems in getting to the point of befriending Bessy. An eighteen stone Jamaican lady, Bessy had to be winched in and out of bed by a sort of crane. She had a back tumour and passed wind constantly with violent percussion. Rude, vulgar, frequently swearing at the patient nurses, she was nevertheless an ardent fan of *Songs of Praise*, and turned the television on as loud as possible each week, accompanying the programme with enthusiastic shouts of 'Hallelujah!' and 'Praise the Lord!' at the top of her voice.

At first I could hardly bear to be in the ward with her. I just wanted peace and quiet, and the loud explosions of every sort from the other side of the room repulsed me. But I knew I was being selfish for she was a very sick woman. Eventually I had the idea of sending Mum out for a big ripe mango (Bessy was on a diet), and from the moment I gave it to her, my heart softened. Her fat face wreathed in huge smiles, she insisted that the nurses crank up the tilt-table so that she was upright, and wheel her over to talk to me. After a while I had an insight into the loneliness and bewilderment of this big woman, and developed a very soft spot for her.

Another fellow patient was a women who resembled a pin. She weighed only about four stone and looked as if she would shatter into little splinters at any moment as she inched her painful way round and round the ward. She was so fragile that she wore a crash helmet on her head and pads on her knees and elbows in case she fell. Twenty-four hours a day she crept along, never speaking a word to anyone, even to the nurse who watched her. She had been referred from an institution and, I believe, returned there after little change at the National.

I did become very close, though, to a girl called Pauline in the next bed. Not much older than me, she had four children who were often in the ward with her husband so that I got quite involved with the whole family. She was suffering from a difficult brain tumour, but was always jolly and optimistic. There were many nights when, after Pauline had fulfilled her motherly instincts by tucking me up snugly, we would lie awake and talk for hours. Pauline was waiting for a major operation which carried many risks of which she was quite aware, but she was incredibly brave and went off to theatre with a smile and a wave. She came back paralysed. It was dreadful to see. Mentally she was undamaged, but she became very miserable and depressed. She was soon taken out of our ward but we kept in touch. Six months later she died. The news hit me very hard.

Friday was the Day of the Week in Gower Ward, the time when Professor Marsden did his ward round. There was always a sense of anticipation and excitement as the nurses got the patients all tidy and ready, rather as you might prepare for a royal visit. For me there was a great feeling of hope as he came and stood by my bed for the first time. A lean, greying man in his fifties he had an air of quiet authority. Many of the other patients in the ward were also waiting for his diagnosis and assessment. He examined me carefully and looked thoughtful.

'We don't seem to have been making much headway with this Algodystrophy, do we?' he said kindly. 'I'd like to do a few tests just to check that we know the whole story. They may not be much fun, I'm afraid,' he added after a pause, 'but hopefully they'll help us to get you sorted out.'

For several days I was wheeled from room to room for a bewildering battery of tests. Electrodes were glued to my scalp, I was wired up to machines, and my reactions to light, sound and sensation were all minutely examined. Electric impulses were passed into my muscles. I was sick, exhausted, and in great pain. The Algodystrophy was confirmed and Professor Marsden told us a little more about the condition, explaining that the pain does not respond to pain-killing drugs, and physiotherapy is ineffective, increasing the pain, but remaining necessary to some extent in order to prevent joints seizing up. There were apparently other drugs that were sometimes effective in treating the condition which he would like to try, and he was hopeful that although it might take a long time, there was a good chance of recovery. He felt, however, that there might be a further rheumatological disorder, and suggested that I be transferred to the Middlesex Hospital which specialised in these conditions.

Tom and I groaned at the thought of another upheaval – we had so much hoped that my stay in the National Hospital would be conclusive and brief. But we were prepared to put up with anything to get me well again. Two weeks after my arrival at the National, I duly moved to Dressmaker's Ward in the fine old building of the Middlesex, and prepared myself for another round of tests.

The atmosphere and character of this ward were very

different from what I had become used to. It was a large and busy mixed ward. The nurses seemed far less warm and demonstrative, having a heavy work load with many severely disabled people suffering from rheumatoid and other types of arthritis. I was tested for all these conditions but none gave a positive result. Even more perplexing was that my right foot was beginning to turn inwards and contract up so that it wouldn't reach the floor if I stood up. Not that I could stand by myself; in fact I couldn't even sit up without help, and it was very stressful to lie prostrate, being looked down upon by everyone. I was beginning to feel, too, like an exhibit in a fair as dozens of doctors and medical students came for a prod or a stare. It was as if I was an interesting piece of flotsam that had been washed up on the seashore and was being examined by scientists. The worst thing was the old suggestion that this was an hysterical condition.

Fortunately there was just one person who took the trouble to sit down and talk to me. One person who believed that I wasn't imagining the pain, and who really supported and encouraged me. She was Dr Lynne Turner-Stokes. We have since become personal friends, but at the time she was the ward's registrar and we called her 'Dr Lynne'.

Tall, attractive and softly-spoken, Dr Lynne had a gentle and sensitive approach to her patients which won the confidence of even the most fearful. Partly because she was also a mother of two small girls we related to each other from the start and she took a great deal of time with me, sitting on my bed, chatting about my family, my dancing and my music. Although she explained to me later that this was a necessary part of trying to establish the origins of my pain, the conversations were friendly and pleasant. A natural friendship grew. It was only much later, too, in a non-professional meeting, that she admitted the degree to which her colleagues suspected my condition to be basically hysterical, and the struggle she'd had to support her conviction that this was not so. She did, though, clear up for me a common misunderstanding of the term 'hysteria'.

In medical jargon, apparently, hysteria doesn't carry the derogatory overtones it does for the layman. An hysterical patient is not necessarily neurotic, emotional and mentally-unbalanced. Nor is he or she consciously faking the condition; that is called malingering. Hysteria merely indicated an unconscious psychological root or component in the production of symptoms of illness. Dr Lynn did admit, however, that there can be a certain 'type' of patient who is more likely to suffer from psychosomatic disease. Together we went through every aspect of my character and background, but we were unable to identify any depressive, insecure or troubled elements in my personality. I had a warm, stable family life to which I was desperate to return and there was nothing for me to gain in illness.

I was fighting desperately to maintain a positive attitude, to believe I would recover, and even this had been seen by some as indifference to my condition (apparently another cardinal sign of hysteria). Dr Lynne, though, seemed to understand and her faith in me was tremendously important for I knew that the doctor at Wimbledon had said in his referral letter that in his opinion I was perfectly able to walk. I had also left that hospital on thirteen different drugs, some of which Dr Lynne told me were antagonistic to each other. She carefully worked out the right combination of medications for me and gradually we cut them down.

As time went on, I did develop a deep appreciation of the exceptional nursing care I received and the skills and knowledge displayed by the doctors in my treatment. It is interesting, though, to observe that some doctors find it hard to accept the limits of their understanding, and the variable effectiveness of their treatments. When a condition fails to respond, some doctors seem to blame the patient rather than going back to the drawing board. I don't think they often appreciate the effects of their attitude unless they find themselves on the other side of the hospital bedcovers. One doctor made no secret of the fact that he considered Algodystrophy to be a condition most commonly found in women of about thirty and with an hysterical disposition.

Yet we have read, in an article published in the *British Journal of Rheumatology* (1987; 26:270) that 'trauma' (which it goes on to describe as physical injury through a fall or accident) 'is the most commonly identified precipitating event.' Old attitudes die hard, but happily the former mode of thinking is giving way to a more enlightened and humble approach as the ripples spread wider from both the acceptance of holistic methods on the one hand, and the advances in medical science on the other.

There seemed little the hospital could do at that point to help me, and I was desperate to be back with the family, so after about two weeks I was allowed home. It was the end of February 1988, and winter seemed reluctant to loosen its hold on a dark, dejected city. Restricted to a wheelchair most of the time, I could not join Tom and the girls when they flew out for the annual skiing holiday in the brilliant sunshine of the Alps. I felt it was important the family carried on as normal, and I knew they could all do with a break, but it was the second year I had been forced to miss the trip and it was hard to say goodbye.

Fortunately we were being helped out at home by a quiet-spoken girl called Katherine. The daughter of my parents' neighbours she fitted in very well and was really more a family friend than a nanny. Having her around stopped me being introspective, but underneath I was longing to be able to tell someone how awful I felt, and share all the thoughts and fears that had arisen while I was in hospital. I missed Penny desperately even though there were lots of other kind, caring friends around, but something within made me very reluctant to discuss my illness. I so much wanted to be normal, and I was determined to eliminate all possibility of a psychological element in my condition. When people called, I talked determinedly, enthusiastically, about their activities and families, made plans, smiled and joked. I hated people to be long-faced and drab, and sometimes I would berate my poor mother for not putting on lipstick, or one of my friends for wearing black or sombre clothes. When you are stuck at home all day almost every day, what people wear and the way they look assume an unnatural importance. They are the only variables in the bleak monotony of getting dressed and undressed, washing and eating.

The passivity of being a mere spectator of my own life frustrated me beyond words. I loathed the word 'disabled'. It carried a ring of dependence and permanence which I resisted with all my strength, and I tried my utmost to do what I could for the children's needs, tying their hair ribbons, helping Mimi with her homework, reading to Georgie. But I knew I wasn't kidding them I was just like every other mum, and it was like a knife in my heart when I caught their look of disappointment or bewilderment when I was unable yet again to share some special event or experience with them. I know Mimi was really embarrassed when I went along to her school play in my wheelchair. I could see she felt horribly conspicuous, as a new girl, with such an odd-looking mother, and I realised with a pang that I shouldn't have gone. Yet I had so much wanted to show her my support and be a 'proper mum'. It seemed either way I couldn't win.

There were worse times, too, when the children were very upset or behaved badly, as children do when they feel insecure or troubled. Then the misery of feeling responsible for their distress would render me inadequate at either discipline or comfort. Besides, physically, I couldn't get up and actually catch hold of them to enforce any instruction or punishment, and then the only recourse was to shout at them, which, as any parent knows, can quickly undermine authority and control. I'm sure there were times when they could have done with a firmer hand as if to give a clearer delineation to their shapeless, ever-changing world. But the tendency for a parent who feels they are failing in one area is, of course, to compensate in another, and, looking back, I can see where episodes of over-indulgence or softness only increased the children's sense of confusion – and my sense of guilt. Mimi's feelings of insecurity were sometimes pathetically revealed. It was a sad evening for me when I heard her pray at bedtime, 'Please God, don't ever let me have an earache, feel sick or have a heart attack.'

No matter how bad things seemed sometimes, we were all united as a family, and Tom and I were very close. I had always appreciated his quick sense of humour, but never more than now, and the laughter we shared often felt better therapy than any of the medical treatments. As if by unspoken agreement, we never looked at the situation negatively. Tom resolutely viewed my illness as a temporary inconvenience though his constant concern was to find ways of relieving my pain and to make the doctors understand the very real and acute nature of that aspect of my problem. His support and faith in me were probably the cornerstone of my determination to recover. Tom prayed with the children each night that I would be made well, and I don't underestimate either the power of those prayers or the beneficial effects to me of such positive commitment and love. With all the medical expertise and determination in the world it can still be very difficult to recover from life-threatening illnesses in a loveless environment.

The doctors at the Middlesex had suggested I came off all pain-killing and anti-inflammatory drugs to see whether my condition could hold its own (and because they suspected a psychological component in my condition?). But as the weeks passed the pain became so intense that it took all my strength and concentration to follow what people were saying and accomplish the simplest of tasks. It was becoming obvious that I couldn't last out much longer at home, but one of the most difficult aspects of this period was the lack of any clear consensus of opinion from the doctors on the next step in the treatment. There were many referrals suggested, appointments made and cancelled, various therapies considered. Tom wrote endless letters, spent hours being passed around hospital telephone exchanges, and kept careful notes on the latest research on Algodystrophy and new drugs being tried.

Yet between the two of us there was the growing conviction that something even more sinister than Algodystrophy was taking hold. The way my right foot was turning in and contracting up steadily was not a symptom of that disease. It was an added strain not knowing what enemy we were fighting. For Tom, on top of doing a demanding job, helping the nanny out with the children, and fielding all the kind but wearing phone calls from friends and family, it was an exhausting routine, and though he always appeared cheerful with me, just sometimes I would catch him at his desk looking haggard and dispirited. It hurt me more than any physical pain.

In April, we bowed to the inevitable and I was readmitted to the Middlesex. A tremor had started in my right leg, and day and night it shook ceaselessly. I felt as if I were constantly running. In hospital it made my bed rattle and creak, and other patients complained of the noise at night. I tried desperately to smother it with the bedclothes. I was plunged into a gruelling routine of hydrotherapy and physiotherapy every day. Even though we all latched on to the slightest sign of improvement, the overall trend, I had to accept, was downwards.

The nurses caring for me were kind in trying to understand what was happening to me. They hadn't seen anything like it before, and made efforts to find some meaning for my ever-increasing disability. Paul, a hospital social worker, was assigned to me. A Jewish man, younger than me I think, he was compassionate and skilled in his counselling. He did his utmost to get me to talk about what was happening and have a good cry! But I had bottled everything up so much by this stage – the effect all the pain was having, the lack of concrete diagnosis, things clearly getting worse, the separation from Tom and the girls, and the admission that I was becoming a disabled person – and although Paul tried valiantly to draw all this out of me, I refused to budge.

It was hard to have any privacy in an open ward so Paul came in triumphant one afternoon to announce he had found a room we could talk in. It turned out to be a store room for the Occupational Therapy Department, full of equipment and appliances, but it just fitted my wheelchair and a seat for Paul. We had some good talks in this incongruous, confined space, but I was still determined not to shed a tear. The outer shell was becoming more and more hard, but the inside was growing ever more hurt and confused, longing to have a rest from the pain. I was aware of the strength of the emotions buried deep down, and I didn't know how I could handle letting them come to the surface.

The hydrotherapy pool was two streets away, and the journey to it was made in the 'milk float', as it was known, a battery-operated van that just fitted two wheelchairs in the back. The trip took at least three quarters of an hour which seemed ridiculous for such a short distance, but the porters weren't allowed to push the patients along the streets to the pool. I never could find out the exact reasons for this, but it was something to do with insurance and accidents en route – and knowing London pavements, I imagined it would be very easy to be tipped out of a wheelchair.

We were collected from the ward at ten o'clock. Frances, my companion in the next bed, could walk so she sometimes set off on her own, or travelled in the milk float if there was room and she wasn't feeling so well. The two of us would then be shoved up the ramp into the van and our wheelchairs anchored to the floor. Then the back would be lifted up and bolted. At this point I felt more like a horse in a horsebox than a bottle of milk, until the vehicle lurched into action and then the two chairs would rock and creak together. The pace was *very* slow, probably four miles an hour at top speed. But it gave us the opportunity to observe the outside world without being stared at ourselves.

The streets surrounding the Middlesex hospital were always alive and busy. There were lots of sandwich bars to supply the local offices, Italian restaurants, and wholesale Indian clothes shops. I always knew when we were nearing our destination as there was a particular dress shop on the corner which had pretty, colourful eastern dresses draped in the window. It was lovely to look at 'normal' things for a bit, and this, coupled with the hope that this might be the day when I would have more control of my body in the therapy session, made the journey quite an adventure. In reality, there wasn't anything remotely normal about travelling in a milk float, strapped to a wheelchair with a tremor in my leg.

Once we had arrived at the physio department, the horsebox would be unbolted and the ramp crashed to the ground. Our chariots (the wheelchairs) were released from their harnesses, and last in, first out. There is a lot of waiting around when you are in a wheelchair. You just have to be patient and rely on the goodwill of the porter, nurse or relative. If people are in a bad mood, or something is troubling them, you can always tell by the way they push you up a pavement kerb.

When we got inside the physio building, there was a lift ride to the basement where the hydro pool was situated, and then the infinitely laborious task of getting undressed again and into a swimsuit. Once there would have been pleasure in such a ritual, or at least the satisfaction of seeing a fit, co-ordinated body preparing for exercise. Now I felt like a beached whale. There were very strict rules regarding safety in a hydro pool – only a certain number in the water at one time, showers before and after, plenty to drink at the end etc. All the regulations were carefully followed and then came the blissful moment of being lowered into the pool. It was the most lovely sensation, sinking into the hot bath-like water. With a physiotherapist behind me and one in front, I would be guided through the waters of Lethe, the Greek river of forgetfulness, and fitted out with floats around my neck and middle. The joy of becoming weightless and letting the water take the strain was wonderful on a spasming body. The physio would guide and hold, gently encouraging, and trying to keep all the 'good' muscles moving to counteract the stiffness which results from being bed-bound. Meanwhile, a surrealistic audience of plastic crocodiles, ducks and dolphins observed us while we exercised – all gifts from grateful patients. After a maximum of thirty minutes, we were given a shower and a drink, and then 'packed', wrapped tightly in a flannel blanket to rest for a while, exhausted. The heat of the water was draining to the little energy one had, but the pleasure of muscles relaxing, and perhaps a glimmer of hope when a spasm reduced a fraction, made it all worthwhile.

They called it Rehabilitation. Sometimes it felt more like annihilation. Hydrotherapy was followed by a long session of physiotherapy. It was a bit like going back to the ballet studio, and I treated the challenge as such. My physio was called Jacky and I would beg her to pull my leg straight. It must – but why wouldn't it? We spent literally hours forcing, stretching, cajoling, persuading – anything to try and correct the offending muscles. A bio-feedback machine, which monitors muscle response, occasionally gave some hope, but any progress required enormous concentration, and the side effects of the drugs and a general feeling of exhaustion made my brain commands barely effective. The lack of control over my body was infinitely depressing. In the vast physio gym, there were bars and huge mirrors. It would have been a lovely place to dance in, yet all I could see looking back at me from the mirrors was an emaciated, twisted creature.

Everyone worked so hard to improve my situation. An occupational therapist made me a really comfortable chair which enabled me to sit upright for the first time in six months – but it caused a frightening increase in the level of pain. Only a few weeks before, after all, the pain specialist had been telling me not to complain as the pain wasn't really there any more. I guessed that most medical opinion concerning me still supported the hysterical diagnosis, but Dr Lynne continued to support me doggedly, convinced that there was a definite organic cause for the condition which they had to uncover. As part of this endeavour, she took me along to a teaching seminar where a number of doctors and medical students reviewed my case. It was a humiliating experience. I felt like an exhibit as they prodded, stared and examined. Then, after much head-scratching, suggestions for the diagnoses were passed around as if I were not only disabled, but deaf, dumb, blind and mentally incapable too. Parkinson's? Wilson's? Huntingdon's diseases? They were enjoying the challenge. A stimulating intellectual exercise. Excuse me, but I'm a person, not a specimen in a test tube. I have feelings and thoughts, hopes and desires. Motor Neurone? Rheumatoid arthritis? Lupus? I'm a human being, not a medical condition. The scientific review continued, but in all the suggestions, the true name of the condition was never mentioned. The doctors retired for their coffee, thoughtful but invigorated. My trolley was wheeled back, rattling, to the ward.

It was May 4th. My thirtieth birthday. I woke up remembering the words of the orthopaedic specialist when I was younger, 'You'll be in a wheelchair by the age of thirty.' I felt numb inside. It was a long day, in which I tried to block out thoughts of the past and the future, and lose myself in the painstaking task of completing my tapestry.

But in the evening, Tom arrived in a defiantly buoyant mood laden down with a box of plastic cups and champagne which he proceeded to hand round, quite illicitly, to everybody on the ward. Then, like beetles out of the woodwork, members of the family and various friends appeared, all resolutely cheerful, and carrying all sorts of touchingly thoughtful presents. Carol, for instance, had found an unusual 'executive toy' – a moving oil picture that was peaceful and relaxing to watch. Tom's sister, Bec, had made a tape of all my favourite songs, for which Tom provided a smart Walkman. Annie brought beautiful notelets so I could write a few lines to the girls each week, and lots of lotions and potions to make me feel feminine. My father, too, brought me some fabulous perfume, whilst Alec added to the festivities by arriving with a helium balloon-in-a-box that he anchored to the end of my bed. Bec raised cheers with an enormous sticky chocolate cake and we ended up having a riotous party to which the nurses kindly turned a blind eye. The night seemed endless and very lonely when they left.

A hopeful visit to see Professor Marsden at the National ended with no further enlightenment, only his words, 'It's a real bastard, isn't it?' ringing in my ears. My right leg was drawing up right across my body and I couldn't make it reach the ground. I was heavily dosed up on sedatives like diazepam and the strong painkiller, omnopon, which made me feel drowsy and even more uncoordinated. Once or twice, I spent the whole of my session down in physio crying with pain, but I wouldn't give up. I *had* to make my body respond. I *had* to get better.

What made me even more desperate to recover was the situation at home. Our kind nanny/friend had had to leave. It was mid-May, and Tom was struggling to cope. Another nanny answered Tom's plea in *The Lady* but couldn't start until the end of the month. The best temporary plan seemed to be for the girls to go and stay with my parents in Hertfordshire for two or three weeks. It was a huge blow, then, when my sister came in to tell me that my father was in hospital having had a suspected coronary. I felt a terrible conflict of emotions – guilt that the extra strain of the children might have provoked the attack, fear that he might not recover from a third coronary, anger and frustration at my helplessness and pity for my little girls who must feel so confused. And Tom. Yet another crisis for him to have to overcome.

I prayed so hard for my father, and next day the news was extraordinary. The ward sister phoned Addenbrookes and apparently he was sitting up in bed quite cheerfully with no remaining evidence of any damage to his heart. It was such a relief that the 'coronary' turned out to be a viral infection, and that he was not seriously ill. Within a few days he would be home. So my mother was able to cope until the new nanny started two weeks later.

Soon after this scare, I was referred to a highly respected elderly consultant specialist. I gritted my teeth throughout the excruciating examination, hoping that from his vast experience he would be able to offer some comfort and clear guidance. But at the end of the examination he was silent.

'Well?' I asked uncertainly. Did he not want to tell me some bad news? 'Is there something you don't want to tell me?'

'Mrs Sheldon,' he replied, running a hand through his grey thinning hair in a gesture of frustration. 'I wish I *did* have something to tell you. I'm very sorry, but all I can say is you think you've seen everything in this business, and then you come across something like this . . .'

And that was that. No diagnosis, no prognosis. No hope – but no despair either. He did suggest that they tried an MUA – manipulation under anaesthetic – to see whether it was possible, physically, to straighten out my contorted leg. We were enthusiastic about this idea. The pain in my hip and leg were now so intense, and the tremor and contraction so strong that I was beginning to wonder if I would ever be straight again, let alone able to sit up properly or walk. Sometimes I felt as if bits of my body might become so brittle and burnt out that they would just fall off and shatter.

A week later, at the end of May, the MUA was carried out. It was a success – or, at least, they managed to straighten out my whole leg and hip under the general anaesthetic. But it only lasted as long as the anaesthetic. We had the comfort of knowing that the condition wasn't irreversible, but it also left me in some confusion. If it was impossible to straighten my leg while awake or even in normal sleep, why could it be achieved in deep unconsciousness? A doctor came and explained to me the involuntary nature of these muscle spasms, and told me of a new drug they wanted to try to release these contractions. Yet another pill. I hated the thought of more medication, more side-effects, more sickness, blurred vision and exhaustion, but I had to play my part, show willing, try to please; I was still tied to that wheel.

To be honest, everyone on the ward was in some fear of the medical staff, particularly of the nurses, strangely enough. Not that there was ever any maltreatment or anything like that. But as patients we sensed a certain competitiveness amongst the nurses, a sort of hierarchy in which the patients were the pawns of battle. We sometimes felt they were interested in good behaviour rather than needs, and we were anxious to win approval, to keep on their good side. I'm sure the nurses were themselves under strain, probably short-staffed, overworked, and pressurised in turn by the doctors, and, perhaps, by the relatives of the patients. But there were times when the ward seemed more like a boarding school than a place of healing and comfort.

Where would I have been without the faithful friends and family who visited, wrote and prayed? Friends who had offices nearby came in during their lunch hours or after work. Dear Jane, my great buddy from Royal Ballet School days, popped in regularly, often bearing the Forbidden Fruit – a Big Mac and a strawberry milkshake! Amelia, too, came and made me laugh. The jokes and news I shared with people like these certainly kept me sane during days otherwise drenched in pain. I was only able to see Mimi and Georgie once a week but Tom usually came round each day after work. This meant he sometimes didn't get home until ten in the evening, ate a hasty supper and went to bed, getting up at the usual commuter hour and leaving the house for work as the girls were still just getting up. He hardly saw the children during the week, and the new nanny had to run the household more or less singlehanded. Perhaps it was my imagination, but each week the girls seemed to show more and more signs of being affected by the situation. Little Georgie was obviously desperate for affection, and saw everyone as a surrogate mum, showering them with hugs and kisses and non-stop chatter. Mimi became steadily more withdrawn and quiet. On one visit she stared at me solemnly and said, 'Mummy, can you ask the doctors to take the frown off your face?' We pretended to laugh but I was mortified. Did I look that miserable? Come on. Smile. Smile. Don't let the mask slip. The strain on everyone seemed to go on for ever.

After the MUA, Dr Lynne felt optimistic enough to suggest putting a plaster-cast on my leg under general anaesthetic after straightening it out completely. The theory was that if the brain once got the message that the leg was meant to be straight, it would stop sending these erroneous signals to the muscles to contract. It sounded a brilliant idea. I was so excited at the prospect of having a straight, still leg once more. By this stage my leg was drawn up almost to my chest and, as well as shaking constantly, occasionally made big jerks and kicks. Quite apart from the fact it was uncomfortable and exhausting, I was acutely embarrassed by it. I still tried to pull my bedcovers up to my neck when certain visitors came and hoped they wouldn't notice the bed shaking.

On the appointed day, I was wheeled down to the theatre feeling confident, even lighthearted. Yet just an hour later, my optimism had turned to terror. As I came round from the anaesthetic, I saw a long white thing flashing past my eyes, and instead of the usual calm, peaceful atmosphere after an operation, there seemed to be commotion and panic all around. As my vision cleared, I realised with growing horror that the white thing was my leg, flailing around uncontrollably and crashing on to the bed. The pain was indescribable.

'Take it off, take it off,' someone was shouting, but I grabbed Dr Lynne's arm.

'No, please leave it,' I gasped. 'We can't give up now. It might settle down in a minute.'

Crash. Crash. I was thrown about the bed as the heavy plaster of paris swung through the air like the boom of a ship. Inside the cast, I could feel the most violent muscle spasms trying to draw my leg back into its foetal position. And then, unbelievably, the plaster started to crack. Now I knew we had come to the end of the road.

Crying, I let them cut the splintered cast off and immediately my leg sprung back across my body like a piece of elastic. Apparently, this time even under the anaesthetic, the jerks and tremors had continued, and now my leg shook and convulsed uncontrollably the whole time. Everyone felt dejected and bemused. But at least this disaster had two small benefits: it convinced the doctors of the organic rather than psychological nature of these movements; and it indicated to them more clearly that the essence of the problem was really neurological, not rheumatological. So back I went to the National Hospital.

The hunt was on to identify the illness, and the search was intense. I spent a whole day, from ten o'clock until four in the afternoon at King's Hospital, undergoing electrical tests in a small dark room banked from floor to ceiling with computers and machines. I was strapped into a sort of execution chair, and wired up to hundreds of electrodes which they glued into my scalp and all over my limbs. All the time my body was shaking and jolting, yet the doctors responded with enthusiasm as they spotted yet another sort of tremor. In all, they identified three main types of spasm. I had a 'dystonic' leg, apparently. They were on to something. My ears pricked up at this new word, but for the time being they didn't want to say too much. On with the stalk. More tests, a brain scan, and yet another neurological case conference with an audience of young medical students.

Today the act they had come to see was an unusual one. A rare phenomenon. News of the freak had got about after the last show, and they were all keen to grab a seat for this matinée performance. None of them had seen anything like it before. Their eyes widened and they craned their necks for a better view. After a brief introduction from the Master of Ceremonies, the audience was invited to comment. Once more a few wild suggestions were thrown about as to the reason for the contortionist's act, and the critics took out their reporter's notebooks to remind them to look up in the library any helpful references.

'Now you won't come across many cases like this . . .' They were talking about me! I felt like the Elephant Man. But although this was a very disturbing exhibit, the subject was *smiling*. (She had years of experience in smiling.) But how could the contortionist smile throughout this excruciating spectacle?

These experiences were distressing, and, I think, psychologically damaging. The patient doesn't seem to be expected to participate in the session in any active way at all. No remarks were addressed to me, and none of the conclusions were discussed with me. At least I had heard most of the suggestions before and knew they were bogus. But once again, I just caught a murmur of acceptance on one point: dystonic spasm. Perhaps we were getting somewhere with all these tests and games. And I had survived so far without too much harm. But the most frightening of all was still to come – the myleogram.

The trolley wheeled me into the very 'high tech' room in the basement of the hospital. By now my right leg was in such tight spasm that it was bent up permanently across my body making lying on my stomach impossible. In fact, being still in any position was out of the question. The technicians came to see me lying on the trolley to decide the best way to conduct the test.

'We need to lie you face down on the bed when we inject the dye into your spine so we can watch the flow up and down the spinal column and into your brain,' they told me (they might have been saying they were going to give me a manicure!) but soon realised it was going to be a difficult task because of my position and the movements that would interfere.

'We've got to have you lying completely still while the dye moves around,' they murmured with some perplexity. I had no idea what was to follow but soon afterwards a jolly young Scottish doctor appeared, holding up a syringe.

'The Professor said you'd probably be needing this,' he told me lightly, as he pumped the liquid into the ever-waiting vent flow in my hand. What joy, what happiness! Pure ecstatic pleasure swept through me, and the Scot laughed.

'Well, that's certainly put a smile on her face!' he exclaimed and called over the nurse and technicians to share my joy. I have no idea what the drug was but I've never felt anything like it in my life. The horror to come now seemed nothing. Everything was beautiful, kind and terribly funny. As they all busied themselves setting up equipment, and working out how on earth they could get me to lie on my front, I laughed and laughed, and hoped this amazing feeling would never leave me.

It took a great deal of time to set up the television screens to monitor the path of the dye, and to find some sort of acceptable position for me, and by the time the syringe was entering my spine the reality of the situation had truly hit me. The effects of the drug had worn off to be replaced by a horrifying, cold, heavy sensation stealing through my back.

The 'table' I was lying on was tipped up and down to allow the dye to move freely up to my brain. I felt it enter my head and the three nurses holding my head tried to be soothing and tell me it would soon be over.

'You must try and lie still,' someone said urgently. But how could I? My leg was jerking uncontrollably. I was half on my side and half on my front with my head in a sort of clamp. Someone was trying to hold down my flailing leg, but that kind of restriction always made it worse. From this position I could only see a great number of legs and white coats around the table with everyone urging me to lie still and for ever reassuring me it would soon be over. I heard a terrifying scream and realised it was me. The liquid was moving around my head until it felt as if it must surely explode.

A voice was close to my ear. Quietly, it said, 'You're doing well. You're being so brave. Keep it up. You're all right.'

I don't remember anything else after that until I woke up drained, exhausted and with a thumping headache in the ward. Only one thing made all this terror worthwhile. After all these tests, at last there was a definite diagnosis. I had Dystonia.

It was a relief, of course, in some ways to be able to give the illness a name, but the problem was now that no one seemed to know much about it. Some of the doctors shook their heads and murmured about what a rare and unusual condition it was, but we pinned our hopes on Professor Marsden. Not that he would cure the condition overnight, but that he would at least give us a straight answer as to the nature of the problem and the best way to treat it.

In his calm, measured way, he gave us the facts. Dystonia

is a syndrome of sustained muscle contractions caused by abnormal brain function, usually in the basal ganglia. The original difficulties over diagnosis earlier this century were caused by an argument over whether Dystonia was a neurological disease or was due to psychological distress. As late as 1970 most patients were referred to psychiatrists in the belief that these curious motor disorders were an expression of an unhappy mind.

Now that its neurological root has been established, the true prevalence of this condition is becoming apparent. Around twenty thousand people in Britain suffer from it, more than the instances of many well-known neurological disorders such as Huntington's Chorea, Motor Neurone disease or Myasthenia Gravia, and about three quarters of those with Multiple Sclerosis. Prolonged muscle contractions are the hallmark of Dystonia, and often they twist the body into characteristic postures, frequently accompanied by rhythmic tremors and jerks. The onset of Dystonia is apparently more frequent in childhood and progresses from affecting just one part of the body (focal Dystonia) to other parts (multifocal Dystonia) or eventually the whole body (generalised Dystonia) in about 60 per cent of children, 35 per cent of adolescents and about 3 per cent of adults. With my mobility deteriorating and the spasms increasing, it looked, then, as if I might be one of the unlucky ones.

When we went on to ask about causes of the condition, Professor Marsden couldn't be very specific. He pointed out that pathological causes were only identified in about 10 per cent of people with focal Dystonias, though there was a strange hereditary component for people who contracted the illness as children. But there are a huge range of metabolic, degenerative and environmental conditions which can result in the symptoms – like viral encephalitis, brain injury at birth, head trauma, toxic exposure to chemicals, side effects of drugs, even wasp stings – and with my history of injuries, illness and drug treatment, it wasn't difficult to see how a chemical imbalance of the brain might have been sparked off.

The important thing now, though, was to establish the ways and chances of recovery. Professor Marsden was positive. There were a number of drugs which could be used, with varying degrees of success depending on the type of Dystonia and he was optimistic that we would soon see an improvement. At the time we didn't press him further but when we received more information from the Dystonia Society, with which he put us in touch, we discovered that there is, in fact, no cure for most types of Dystonia; all that can be offered is the treatment of symptoms. Apart from this, some patients with Dystonia may experience a spontaneous improvement of their movement disorder. Remission could, theoretically, last for years, though subsequent relapses are common. In practice, it seems that sustained remission is almost unheard of, and temporary improvements are more likely.

At this stage, though, Tom and I were just glad to be launched on a clear course of treatment. I was to be put on a constant epidural drip for a week to administer a particular drug to control the spasms. It was incredibly uncomfortable to try and be immobile on my side with my legs shaking all the time, but after a few hours my left leg became much more still and only my right leg kept twitching. It was a wonderful feeling to have relief from pain in at least one part of my body for the first time in many months. I felt like shouting, 'Hooray!'

The elation was short-lived. In the evening Mum and Dad had come to see me and we were deep into family news when suddenly my chest went so tight I just couldn't breathe. I pulled frantically at my necklace, gasping for air, when the whole of my body seemed to go into an enormous spasm. One hand curled up into a fist and the other into a contorted claw. In horror my mother shouted for the nurses, and instantly figures were rushing round the bed, the curtains were flung across, and the anaesthetist fought desperately to disconnect the epidural whilst I convulsed wildly on the bed. I felt as if I would be strangled by my own muscles, and although I was completely conscious, I couldn't communicate at all. I really thought I was going to die. At last the anaesthetist stopped the pump, and gradually the spasm released its grip leaving me drenched and exhausted, but most of all dismayed. My hands seemed now fixed in their contorted positions.

My poor parents. I was as much upset that they had witnessed all that as I was about the experience itself. Some sort of fit, the doctors said, caused perhaps by the drug in the epidural going too quickly into my brain. Although I hadn't appreciated the difficulties, it seemed that administering this drug carried an unavoidable risk. In order for the treatment to be effective, as high a dose as possible has to be given, but the problem is that each person has a different level of tolerance to the drug, and a hospital can't know that danger point beforehand. In this case the gamble hadn't paid off. Yet again the treatment had to be changed, and with a sinking heart I learnt I had to be transferred to the Middlesex once more for a course of twenty daily nerve blocks.

It was the middle of July, and hot and stuffy in the centre of London. While the schools closed and families set off on their summer holidays I joked I was off for a luxury stay at a health farm. But underneath I felt very low as I had some idea of the regime these blocks would involve. The harsh reality was being starved every morning for three weeks in order to be given a general anaesthetic. These psoas blocks, as they were called, sometimes proved very effective in removing all pain and reducing the tremor in my leg for a few hours. Although my foot was still inverted and drawn up, for a short while each day I could imagine what it was like to be normal again. But on other days, the blocks didn't seem to work at all. Not only did the tremors and jolts remain as bad, but with growing dismay I had to admit that my claw-like hand was progressively hurting more and more. At first I didn't even tell Tom, not until I had come to terms with what I suspected was the grim truth. The disease was spreading through my body.

For a while I felt bewildered. Despite all the prayers, all the faith, all the apparent promises from God about my healing, I was getting steadily worse. It would have been much harder, I'm sure, if my family and friends had given any indication that they shared my fears, but they all remained resolutely strong and confident that I would recover. So I was helped through the times of confusion and doubt, and learnt gradually to trust in God's promises and power, instead of concentrating on my ever-changing symptoms. A bit like Peter, I suppose. I was fine so long as I didn't look at the waves.

What kept me going more than anything was reading the Bible. I expect all the other patients thought I was a crank, poring over the Psalms every day, but for me it was better than hiding in a Mills and Boon novel or in the astrology section at the back of magazines:

> He who dwells in the shelter of the Most High will rest in the shadow of the Almighty. I will say of the Lord, 'He is my refuge and my fortress, my God in whom I trust.' (Ps 91: 1–2)

Even in the busy open ward, I knew I was surrounded by God's protection and love. The doctors and nurses were doing all they could but I felt my real hope lay in the Lord:

> Surely He will save you from the fowler's snare and from the deadly pestilence. He will cover you with his feathers, and under His wings you will find refuge; His faithfulness will be your shield and rampart. (Ps 91: 3–4)

Reading these lines in Psalm 91 helped me overcome my initial fear of Dystonia. However frightening this 'deadly pestilence' sounded, I knew that God was able to save me from it, and give me courage and faith even if, humanly speaking, there appeared little hope:

> You will not fear the terror of night nor the arrow that flies by day nor the pestilence that stalks in the darkness, nor the plague that destroys at midday. (Ps 91: 5–6)

So God knew all about the terror of darkness, the dreadful feeling of isolation and fear that can overwhelm you in the long, pain-filled hours of sleeplessness. And the horrors of all the tests and treatments that filled the day. Every second, every thought, every sensation was watched over by Him. And as a mother myself, there couldn't have been any image more meaningful for me than that of the Lord gathering me under his wings like a bird would cover her young:

> 'Because he loves me,' says the Lord, 'I will rescue him; I will protect him, for he acknowledges my name. He will call upon me, and I will answer him; I will be with him in trouble, I will deliver him and honour him. *With long life will I satisfy him and show him my salvation.*' (Ps 91: 14–16)

Again and again, I read those words. Each time something seemed to burn in my heart, as if there was something precious and personal in this promise. There, quietly, slowly, they generated a belief in my Lord's love and healing purpose for me which nothing could extinguish. People later called me brave and strong. But it wasn't really that. The faith and strength everybody else saw were, in fact, like divine gifts; I trusted Him, but it was He who gave me the courage and will never to give up.

Not that there weren't times when I felt like doing so. After the seventh nerve block, I had another frightening convulsion or fit. I was engulfed by total body spasms, unable to speak, hardly able to breathe. People were rushing, machines wheeled in, and finally the oblivion of an injection which knocked me right out. When I came round, I was on a heart monitor, and they kept me in the recovery room all afternoon instead of putting me back in my normal bed. But that night the fit struck again. This time nobody realised what was going on as I was powerless to attract anyone's attention until a doctor happened to come into the ward. Then there was pandemonium once more and a voice shouting 'Do you mean she's been like that for half an hour and nobody called us? Somebody, quickly! Telephone her husband!' I tried desperately to beg them not to worry Tom with a night-time phone call, but I couldn't speak. Then nothing.

That night I was given a 'special' – a nurse who sits by you all the time just watching all the monitors. The next day I felt completely drained and in terrible pain. Everyone treated me with gentleness and there was no block that day. Apparently it was the dosage of the drug which had yet again proved toxic. After these experiences the hospital seemed to have worked out what level I could tolerate, and the rest of the blocks were administered without mishap. But to our dismay, the chemical balance of the brain seemed to be further disrupted by these fits. From now on, a pattern of frightening full body spasms began to establish itself.

Yet more drugs were given to me, notably benzhexol and the L-dopa drugs used to treat Parkinson's, plus various muscle relaxants like diazepam. All together they made me feel pretty much like a zombie, lethargic, confused, sick and depressed, with frequent headaches and blurred vision. The physiotherapy continued, and in some respects I seemed to be making progress as my leg had straightened out considerably and I could just about get my toe to the ground, even managing to hop a few steps on crutches. At the same time, though, my hand, wrist and elbow were getting steadily worse so that even lifting a cup was difficult. Deep down I felt I was simply swapping one set of problems for another.

It helped, therefore, to have just one immediate practical aim – to get out of hospital, and restore some sort of family equilibrium. Nannies had come and gone, and so had Mimi's sixth birthday (kind Granny had given her a party, but it grieved me a lot that I hadn't been the one to ice her cake and help her open her presents). I had to get home again.

On August 19th, armed with wheelchair, crutches, and a formidable cocktail of drugs, I was allowed out of hospi-

tal. I had been there for sixteen weeks. Everyone was jubilant. No one voiced the doubts and worries that perhaps
we all felt. Could I sustain the improvement, or would my
condition deteriorate?

7

The Dying Swan?

Initially it was exhilarating to be at home, to see the children again, to have the joy of holding them, and kissing them every day after months of once-weekly meetings. But any happy thoughts I might have had about picking up the reins again, and re-establishing the domestic status quo, were quickly revealed as naive and impractical. Very soon I had to accept the fact that I wasn't a steadily-improving convalescent; I was a severely disabled person – or, at least, that was the truth but I'm not sure if I ever fully accepted it! For much of the day I could only lie on the sofa or bed. It was still the nanny or friends who took the children for walks, cooked their tea, disciplined their bad behaviour. It was very hard lying upstairs and hearing the sound of either laughter or tears, and not being part of it.

A few days after coming out of hospital Tom arranged to take me shopping in Sutton, and he might as well have been offering a trip to Disneyland so excited did I feel! Yet the stark reality meant that I returned home subdued and depressed. It is one thing to be ill and disabled in hospital; that's how people expect you to look, and you are perfectly 'normal'. Take a doped-up, disabled young woman out on to the streets in a wheelchair, and the world turns and stares. It was a great shock to be treated like a freak. I had taken a lot of trouble over putting on make-up and wearing (oh bliss!) attractive 'real' clothes. Did I still look abnormal? Catching sight of myself in a shop window, I realised with a start that I did. Thin, shaking, twisted, heavy eyed.

How could Tom bear to be out with a wreck like that? I lost all interest in the colour and bustle which at first I had found so stimulating and enjoyable.

'Can we go home now, Tom?' I asked quietly. 'I – I'm feeling very tired suddenly.' From then on, I rarely went out, except to places like Wimbledon Common with the family, where I wouldn't be ogled at by crowds, and cause embarrassment to the children.

And so the weeks passed and autumn faded gradually into winter. Some days were better than others, and once or twice I pushed away my crutches and managed to walk a few steps by myself. But the next day, I might be racked by awful spasms and tremors, unable to get out of bed.

Even though we were constantly surrounded by practical support, prayers and encouragement, the pressures were relentless. Tom had the wearying task of fielding all the endless telephone calls from well-wishers anxious for the latest medical update, and he spent almost every moment at home after work, repeating depressing details of my physical condition. This might have proved too much even for Tom, had it not been for two new developments.

First, Tom, who had been working with a large firm of surveyors, was offered the opportunity of setting up a development company with one of his clients. He had always wanted to be his own boss, and he leapt at the chance. By October he was able to open his new office in Piccadilly. This coincided with our ninth wedding anniversary, and it was a special day for both of us when he took me to see his new office, and then to dinner at The Inn on the Park Hotel – wheelchair and all. It was so good to see his enthusiasm and happiness. It was a tacit game of pretence we willingly played for each other's sake.

The second significant event was the fact that Tom's parents, finding their big, rambling house less convenient now for their needs, were busy converting a Victorian barn and outbuildings on their farm into a beautiful new home. In the spring they were going to put the house on the market. Until now, we couldn't even have considered buying it, but Tom's new business venture gave us the opportunity to move to a larger house and leave Wimbledon which Tom, in particular, was finding ever more claustrophobic.

Tom, naturally, was very keen on the idea. He had grown up in the house and loved the countryside around. For my part, I could see the many advantages in the obvious support his parents would be able to give, and his sister, Polly, also lived in the village with her family, but inwardly I dreaded the practical aspects of coping with a major house move from a wheelchair. Nor could I imagine how I would manage with three floors of Victorian/ Edwardian idiosyncrasy and four acres of garden. But plans nevertheless went ahead. Professor Marsden had actually indicated that I might never make a full recovery, and Tom, with a man's long perspective, felt sure that this was the right decision for the whole family.

I felt very sad, almost bereaved, at the thought of leaving the secure and sheltered haven of Wimbledon where I was surrounded by friends who had known us for several years. Here I was loved and accepted as I was. To leave seemed to me like letting go of a lifebelt, and I felt daunted at the prospect of trying to make new friends. I had felt low many times during my illness but had never lost the will to fight or the belief that I would recover. Now, feelings of despair filled me, and I realised with a sense of shock that the bottles of pills lined up on my bedside offered a sinister and horribly attractive way out of this mess which was causing everyone so much trouble. Before it was too late, I managed to confess these destructive thoughts to Tom, and he seemed to recognise at once that something was beginning to give way inside me.

This cry for help brought one benefit. It broke my shell of invincibility, making everyone aware, including myself, that I needed to be real with people. So as the winter brought a fresh onslaught of pain and tremor, it wasn't so hard to admit that the disease was spreading. Strong spasms were beginning to attack my arms, shoulders, neck and chest. My shoulders started to draw up, and slowly, insidiously, my head started to turn to one side and drop down. I felt very unwell. The side-effects of increased drugs were dreadful, and made the situation even harder for the family. I would often feel agitated and confused, my eyes wouldn't focus properly, and I would sometimes sit staring at an object, such as a letter, for ages before I remembered what it was I was meant to do with it. I was given a collar to support my head but it continued to twist, and my hands, legs and foot completed the corkscrew.

Then the doctors began talking about a new drug, still in its experimental stages but producing encouraging results for some in the alleviation of their muscle spasms — botulinum toxin. It sounded very dubious. I knew botulism was a type of potentially fatal food poisoning, and there had been a major outbreak in Birmingham in 1978 when two people actually died after eating contaminated tinned salmon. What made me even more wary was that it was Porton Down, the former microbiology Defence establishment, which had become the centre for the production of this potent substance. My fears were allayed, however, when I was told that in 1979 Porton Down became the Centre for Applied Microbiology and Research (CAMR). It was also pointed out to us that all medicines are poisonous if taken in the wrong manner or amount. The clinical trials at Moorfields Eye Hospital and the National Hospital for Nervous Diseases had shown that many Dystonia sufferers had substantial benefit from injections of this toxin. Botulinum toxin works by blocking the release of a neuromuscular transmitter, that is, a chemical substance which bridges the gap between the nerve cell and the muscle it actuates. There could be side-effects including drooping eyelids or double vision, and, if injected into the neck, some difficulty in swallowing and breathing. But all these effects should be mild and temporary, wearing off after two to three months as the nerve junctions re-grow.

After weighing up the pros and cons, we thought we might as well give it a try. After all, it seemed I had very little to lose. The toxin was injected into the calf muscle of my right leg and although it didn't make me feel any more appreciably unwell, neither was there a very obvious improvement in the posture of my leg and foot. In the New Year, my head and neck were so bad that a series of injections were given into that area. The spasms and distortion did begin to decrease after a week or so, but I felt ill.

Tom and I were attempting to keep some semblance of social life going. Before I had become ill we used to go to the theatre, cinema and ballet regularly, and I often felt guilty that Tom now had to lead such a boring, mundane life, deprived of the relaxation and interests he used to enjoy. So when Tom suggested we take his partner and wife, whom I had never met, out to dinner at a smart London restaurant, I was keen to go, and absolutely determined that my condition wouldn't alter the evening in any way. Tom had made a conscious decision to play down my illness with work colleagues, so they were completely unprepared for the nature and extent of my disability. I could see the sense of shock and pity on their faces when we were introduced, but they covered it valiantly, and we had a good lighthearted evening, despite the fact that I could eat very little and sitting at a table for three hours was agony.

The annual dinner at Tom's Yacht Club was less enjoyable. In that crowded dining room, I was acutely aware that I had become something to gawp at. I managed to hobble in on my crutches, looking relatively normal, but as soon as I sat down my right leg sprung up as if on elastic, and clamped itself across my body. The clattering of my knife and fork on the plate as the tremors hampered my eating caused further stares. The embarrassment was almost tangible, and we left soon after I had spilt most of my coffee on the prim white tablecloth.

In March, the botulinum toxin treatment was stepped up. Over the next six weeks, I was given eight more injections, including three on one day. The improvement was soon obvious to everyone, and I was straighter than I had been in almost three years. But the poison was also taking its toll. I was becoming very weak. It took me an hour and a half to get dressed in the morning, and then all I could do was lie, exhausted, on my bed for most of the morning.

Although I dragged myself around the house on my crutches as much as possible, especially when the children came home from school, the reality was I could do almost nothing for them except lie on the sofa and talk – though even that became more and more of an effort. No one really dared to admit at first that my voice was beginning to fail, but within a few weeks it was reduced to little more than a whisper. As the botulinum attacked the spasms in my neck and shoulders, so swallowing became increasingly difficult, and I had to start eating puréed food like a baby. Meanwhile my arms grew so weak that eventually I couldn't even lift a coffee cup.

I was utterly dependent, and even after all this time it embarrassed me greatly to be so helpless in front of the nanny who was a difficult girl despite her competence, often moody and withdrawn. We were due to move down to Kent very soon, in the middle of April, a stressful enough event at the best of times, but in these circumstances it was frightening to think how reliant the whole family had become on a young girl we had known for barely six months. Then, just a week before the move, when our house in Wimbledon lay in dismembered chaos about our ears, our nanny, deciding that she didn't want to move to the country, handed in her resignation.

This news hit me like a physical blow. Suddenly I fell forward through the kitchen door and my body was seized by violent, uncontrollable spasms. My head was thrown back and my hands clawed the air while my legs thrashed wildly against the door frame. I wasn't unconscious, but it was impossible to communicate, and all I could hear were wild screams which I knew, with mounting terror, must be coming from me. Tom tried frantically to buffer my bleedings shins from the door with cushions, whilst he dialled urgently for the doctor.

In the middle of all this frenzy, there came a little voice from the landing and Mimi's pale, frightened face stared down at us. 'Daddy, is Mummy going to be all right?'

Tom's features contorted in anguish before he looked up and replied reassuringly, 'Mummy's just fallen down, darling, but she'll be fine in a minute. Just slip back to bed and I'll be up to kiss you very soon.'

Mimi obviously wasn't convinced. She lingered for a moment, watching the writhing figure with fascinated horror, before running for the safety and warmth of her bed. Gradually the spasms grew less, and by the time the doctor arrived with a sedative, Tom had carried me gently upstairs.

From Mimi's subdued, withdrawn behaviour next morning I knew witnessing my attack had gone very deep with her. Over the next few months I realised that there was a lot of fear, anxiety, even anger and rejection, which were being pushed far underneath. I felt powerless to help her. I felt guilty at the disruption the coming house move would cause her, not least the change from her little school in Wimbledon to a large day school for girls in Sevenoaks. She would be entering mid-year, stressful at the best of times. Dear little Mimi. She was so loving to me, and thoughtful of her young sister over whom she clucked and fussed like a mother hen – buttering her toast, reading her stories, encouraging her to be a 'brave girl' and not to be naughty. But she often looked grave and preoccupied, far, far older than her years, and I longed desperately to see her lighthearted and carefree, enjoying life instead of shouldering its burdens. If it was just the pain, I think I could still have hidden from the children how bad things had become, but these total body spasms were happening more and more frequently, almost every day, and I could no longer shield the children from the horror of the disease.

I remember little of the move to Kent. I was heavily sedated much of the time, and only dimly aware of the enormous furniture lorry, and a great deal of activity and kindness from all our friends in Wimbledon. Tom's parents, Rodney and Pam, couldn't have been more helpful and supportive, and our nanny reluctantly agreed to stay on for a few weeks until we got settled in. It was wonderful to have so much space, and the children were excited and enthusiastic about exploring all the rooms and the large, rambling garden.

I felt disorientated and lonely — during the moments that I was able to think at all. Gradually, breathing became such an effort that I had to lie in bed with an oxygen mask on most of the day and night. Added to this, the double vision and blurred focus were now so severe that reading was out of the question. Professor Marsden and the neurologist I was seeing at the Atkinson Morley Hospital for the botulinum injections could offer no further encouragement. We all knew they were giving as aggressive a dose of botulinum as they dared. It was our last line of defence.

People such as my parents, Annie and Giles, Penny and Virginia, seemed unshakeable in their belief that God *would* heal me, though I learnt afterwards just how much that faith had been forged in a furnace of brokenness and sorrow. As for Tom, it would have been so easy for him to think bitterly, 'Why me?' Yet his constant response was simply, 'Well, why not me?', and that humble acceptance of the situation played a large part in preventing anger and resentment. He was also very good at looking neither forward nor back, but just taking each day as it came, and in that way probably conserved a lot of mental and emotional energy. He was always positive and encouraging, and we were very much in love. It was amazing how, even in the worst times, there was so much laughter and happiness between us.

Not that Tom wasn't under a lot of pressure to give up. He knew now that there was no real medical cure for Dystonia, that all the treatment was aimed at alleviating the symptoms. Professor Marsden had been very honest and practical with Tom, and had admitted that although they were giving the best treatment available, at the end of the day all the drugs might be of limited help, and we must just 'let the good Lord take His course.' I learnt later that some people involved in my illness were horrified at the effects of the drugs, and thought darkly that if I survived the Dystonia, I might well die of the treatment. Certainly the botulinum toxin seemed to be drawing me inexorably closer to death as I steadily became weaker and thinner by the day.

A more subtle pressure was the urgent advice of others to seek alternative treatment. Some people were amazed at what they saw as our stubbornness and stupidity in not exploring every possible avenue to get me well again. Acupuncture, reflexology, homeopathy – there were few therapies that weren't urged upon us by friends who felt we really had nothing to lose. For my part, I had certain reservations about many of these alternative treatments, and certainly no strength or energy to follow them through.

It was much harder for Tom. He had a weighty sense of responsibility for me. At this time he had injured his back slightly, and was seeing an osteopath who was very keen on alternative treatment. She urged Tom to send a lock of my hair to an 'electrician' living in Hammersmith who apparently had very good results with people suffering from neurological illnesses. Tom had to admit he was keen to try as he felt at this stage it couldn't do any harm. But I was adamant. The osteopath even suggested Tom should snip off a piece of hair while I was asleep and send it off in an envelope without my knowing, but Tom knew that would undermine the complete trust we had always had in one another. So he finally abandoned all thought of it, and later had cause to be very grateful that we hadn't gone down that particular road.

Not that he had much time to consider other courses of action. Sorting out help at home was a never-ending, time-consuming task and he spent hours writing ads, making phonecalls, conducting interviews and explaining the ropes. When I spotted an advertisement he had placed in *The Lady*, it filled me with anguish and remorse:

Desperate dad seeks wonder woman (twenty-two plus) to assist disabled mum with two girls (six and a half and three and a half) and have sole charge of running home . . .

It was May and the nanny who had been with the family for the past nine months was finally about to leave. We wondered if it would be better to look for a more mature

woman, particularly as I was now more or less bed-ridden.
Perhaps more of a mother-figure would enable the children,
for whom my heart ached, to express their feelings and
give them a greater sense of security and comfort. I realised
now that while children appear very resilient and adaptable
even in quite shocking or desperate situations, a lot goes
on underneath which only comes to the surface later.

The woman we eventually took on came with excellent
references, and Tom was particularly delighted as she was
meant to be a very good cook! We had hoped I would be
able to show her the ropes and establish a good relationship
between us all, but by the time she started at the beginning
of June my condition had deteriorated so much that I was
taken back into the National Hospital. Tom was left high
and dry with a new housekeeper – and her cat, around
which life seemed to revolve. This was only one indication
of the difficulties ahead, so it was with enormous relief
after she chose to leave a month later that Tom answered
the phone 'out of the blue' to Claire, who had helped us
out before. She was home from University for the summer
holidays and had no job plans – did we know anyone who
needed a nanny? Tom leapt at the suggestion and offered
Claire her old job back. The girls were so excited at the
prospect of her return and Tom was relieved that the nanny
problem was solved for another two months.

For much of the coming weeks, I was hardly aware of
what was going on and how ill I really was, so part of what
follows is pieced together from what I have since been told
by the people who so faithfully supported and cared for
me. When I was readmitted into the National, I was taken
straight into the Intensive Care Unit with severe breathing
problems and malnutrition. I was immediately put on to a
nasal food drip and on increased oxygen. I was almost too
weak to move, and it needed two people to enable me to
sit up for a sip of water. My body was hideously contorted,
both legs drawn up, arms at right angles, one hand in a
claw, the other a fist, head pulled to one side. The pain
was fearful.

But the full body spasms were the worst. My legs would

retract up even further and tangle together. My arms found their way behind my back, twisted and bent. My head pulled right back, arching my spine, until I felt I was being suffocated. When the spasm was over, I tried to joke that I felt (and looked) like a stranded beetle on its back. These attacks could occur at any time and without warning. I might be talking with someone or just lying still. The ferocity and power of these body spasms was overwhelming. The nurses were so sensitive towards me, and would quickly pull the curtains around my bed for privacy as the beetle writhed and twisted on the bed. I recall Tom gently untangling my arms and legs and coaxing them back in front of my body again. Any force or quick movement in an attempt to regain some sort of normal position would be met by fierce resistance, and consequently the spasm would last even longer. Even with years of ballet training behind me, I couldn't believe the weird, contorted positions my body got itself into. The power in the muscles pulling in all the wrong directions was incredible. It was also exhausting, as if, in those few minutes, I had spent a full two hours in the ballet studios. The only relief from this torture was my old friend, the drug midazolam, which wrapped me in a deep sleep and glorious oblivion.

For over a week, the medical staff battled to stabilise my condition, whilst outside the hospital, hundreds of others battled in prayer. The network of support which had sprung up was quite remarkable. Virginia, who had continued her encouragement towards me ever since that first meeting at HTB, had got dozens of people praying for me. She had a strong sense that God was going to heal me. A few weeks before, she had told me of a vision, a picture in her head, which she had seen of a brandy goblet of plain glass being deeply cut to reveal a spectrum of sparkling lights. She felt God was saying that this sickness, which was cutting so deeply into me, would reveal His glory to me and through me, specifically to the family.

More and more we all had this conviction that God had a far greater plan than just healing my body. In fact, we realised that God's healing *always* involves more than that.

I had already seen that He wanted me to learn how to be honest with myself and those around me instead of hiding my feelings. I had growing understanding that I was loved and accepted by God and by others – not for what I could achieve or the performance I could give, but for who I was. Now I was learning just how great and gracious God always is when He deals with us, that there is an extravagance in His love to us which overflows as blessing into other people's lives.

Soon afterwards, Virginia had another picture, this time of a gnarled and twisted olive tree bearing a huge crop of olives, and with the picture she received the words, 'Through the twisting of your body you will bear much fruit in your life for me.'

And now, as I lay crippled and dying in intensive care she saw a broken jar of precious perfume, such as Mary used to anoint the feet of Jesus. As the costly ointment was pouring out, she felt God saying, 'Through the breaking of your body, my fragrance will fill your house.'

Weak and helpless as I was, these promises gave me strength and hope. This sort of encouragement was coming from all around me. It was almost as though God was mobilising a huge army to fight on my behalf. Annie, for example, had asked Giles and his friend Ed to organise a network of constant prayer support for me, and they got several committed Christians, some who didn't even know me and would probably never meet me, to agree to fast and pray every Friday for my healing. The whole group possessed a total conviction that God was going to heal me. For example one person wrote to Ed to say that God had led her to Mark II: 23–24:

'I tell you the truth,' said Jesus, 'if anyone says to this mountain, "Go throw yourself into the sea," and does not doubt in his heart, but believes that what he says will happen, it will be done for him. Therefore I tell you, *whatever you ask for in prayer, believe that you have received it, and it will be yours.*'

Somebody else said that she had been given the verse, Luke 1: 45: 'Blessed is she who has believed that what the Lord has said to her will be accomplished.'

Someone else was struck by 2 Corinthians 10: 3–4: 'For though we live in the world, we do not wage war as the world does. The weapons we fight with are not the weapons of the world. On the contrary, they have divine power to demolish strongholds.'

The battle between good and evil in the world was never so apparent to these praying friends as now. My part in the battle was simply to stay alive! I know now though, the extent to which others did take on the powers of darkness, and through their faithful prayer and fasting helped to deliver me from destructive forces. For example, at a Full Gospel Businessmen's meeting in the City, an evangelistic fellowship of Christian men, where Ed had told about my situation, a man who knew nothing about me had a picture of a scorpion lying on its back being slowly poisoned by the sting in its own tail, and at the same time he felt a terrible pain in his head, neck and shoulders. The whole group prayed against the insidious destructive power suggested by this picture.

I believe that if there hadn't been this type of 'specialist' prayer, as well as all the other types of prayer support and help – spiritual, moral and practical – I would never have recovered. If illness is a battle, then each division of the army is vital to the success of the whole operation, and, indeed, every single soldier has his unique role to play. Individual recognition or importance doesn't come into it; the purpose of all the effort is simply to win the war. Sometimes certain people seem to play a more spectacular role, but in fact, their contribution is only possible because of the steady, unselfish preparation or back-up of others. Even in the bloodiest moments of my battle for life, everyone seemed to recognise these principles, and amongst all the many groups involved, there was appreciation of one another. Those of us who believed in God had no doubt as to the ultimate good that He would bring out of all this and while we were convinced that the suffering wasn't sent by Him, we felt sure that He was going to use it to reveal His love and power. Again, it was Virginia who had a picture which seemed to convey this purpose so movingly. She saw a Columbia Films logo of a woman in white standing on a mountain top bearing a lighted torch of fire in her upheld hand, and seemed to hear the words:

> I will raise her up. Through her suffering I will reveal my glory as I did through my Son's suffering. She is to be crowned with my glory and to be lifted high to be my witness. All things will be in my hand, and in my timing, for I am the Lord who heals and delivers. I will use you [Virginia] in part, and others in part, but my Body on earth will be manifested in power in Julie's life.

Perhaps most miraculous of all was the incident involving my brother Alec. He wouldn't have called himself a committed Christian, yet he was suddenly woken up in the middle of the night by an audible voice which said, 'Don't worry. Julie will be fine.'

Terrified and amazed, he sat bolt upright in bed, in no doubt at all who had spoken. He didn't sleep a wink for the rest of the night in case the Almighty addressed him again! But afterwards he had as much faith as the rest of us that God would do as He had said.

Perhaps with all these promises, it sounds as if there should have been no problem believing that God would heal me. But every single one of these pictures and messages came not only when I was very, very ill, but when my condition was still deteriorating. There was no medical or visible reason for confidence, or even hope, yet everyone had it. God had indicated that He had the timing of everything in His hand. By an extraordinary 'coincidence', it happened that as I lay swamped by drips and tubes and monitors in intensive care, Canon Jim Glennon, an Australian Anglican minister with a world-wide ministry of healing, was paying a visit to London. First he visited Annie's church where she had the opportunity of speaking to him about me, and then he went to the London Healing Mission where Virginia was able to ask him to come and pray for me. Virginia had clung doggedly to the words she had been given, 'I will not let my holy one see decay,' and when she visited me that week she prayed the words she felt were for me, 'Arise, little girl.' But she felt in her heart that she had done all she could for me (she had even borrowed Andy Arbuthnot's oil and anointed me!) and yet she had to accept that the facts were I was still dying. It was time, evidently, for God to bring in someone else and here, remarkably, was a man with a quite exceptional gift of faith for healing. Jim Glennon had apparently been moved by my story and was glad to visit me on Wednesday 14th June.

I'd just been brought out of the Intensive Care Unit and placed in my old bed next to Lynne who was also suffering from Dystonia. Virginia came and sat by my bed followed by a grey-haired, tall, slightly stooping man.

'Julie, I'd like you to meet Jim Glennon,' she said, and he reached forward to touch my bent, curled-up hand. I was in a great deal of pain and heavily drugged so it was hard to focus and concentrate, but I was immediately aware of his quiet, gentle manner, and the deep compassion in his voice. He didn't ask about my illness at all, but instead talked a little of his trip to England and then asked about Mimi and Georgie whose photograph he had seen on my locker. Looking back, it was as if he was wanting to turn my thoughts away from the negative side of my situation, towards all the good things left to live for — which suggests, I suppose, that a person's state of mind, whether hopeful or despairing, plays just as important a part, perhaps, as the actual prayer for healing.

As my concentration span was so short, and talking very tiring, Jim soon suggested that we pray. Virginia volunteered they swapped places so he was nearer me (she told me later that she had a ridiculous feeling that the closer he was, the more likely his prayers would work!) but he declined. Very simply and with quiet authority he began to pray that my twisted body would be healed. It was hard to follow what he was saying, but afterwards Jim wrote a passage of Scripture on a scrap of paper and pinned it to the side of my locker. ' "EVEN WHEN WE ARE TOO WEAK TO HAVE ANY FAITH LEFT, GOD REMAINS FAITHFUL TO US AND WILL HELP US." Paul.'

He wrote in bold capital letters so that I could just make out the words. He followed this with a positive declaration:

THANK YOU, FATHER, YOU ARE HEALING ME NOW.
THANK YOU, FATHER,
THANK YOU, JESUS,
THANK YOU, SPIRIT.
THANK YOU, FATHER, VIRGINIA IS BELIEVING FOR ME TOO.
AMEN.

I felt momentarily that I had been in the presence of someone special. I wanted to ask so many questions but felt too weak to put them together. I don't think I even remember them leaving. I probably just drifted into sleep.

A short time later I woke up and instantly felt able to sit up. Just a strong thought that I *knew* I could sit up. And I did! Yet just that morning when I had asked for a drink of water, it had taken Mum and a nurse to lift me up and forward to have a sip. Now here I was in the afternoon sitting up unaided. 'This is terrific!' I thought, but at the time didn't put two and two together that this might be a direct answer to prayer. That evening Giles arrived to find me sitting up in bed, beaming.

'What's been happening?' he asked, amazed at the transformation from the curled up shape huddled in bed he had seen just the day before.

'I don't know,' I replied (oh ye of little faith!) 'but I'm feeling good!'

Later I was told Giles rushed home and telephoned Tom to tell him of the improvement. Tom hadn't been able to visit me that day for the first time in ages, and hardly dared get his hopes up too much. There had been setbacks and counter-attacks before, so far from stopping the prayer and becoming euphoric, everyone redoubled their efforts, asking for the improvement to be sustained.

The following day, after the morning's exhausting ritual of bathing, the physio came round, ready to encourage and try to find some normal control in my spasming limbs.

'I feel like trying to walk today,' I announced. She looked very surprised, but pleased, and simply reminded me that I'd been in bed a long time so I would feel pretty weak. But she made no attempt to thwart my efforts.

My crutches had been gathering dust behind the bed. I managed to sit on the edge of the bed with the help of the physio and attach the crutches to my bent arms. I'd already announced to Lynne in the next bed my intentions so I felt there was no going back. Crippled and helpless herself, she watched round-eyed as I prepared to launch out. I felt very excited as I was helped to my feet (well, foot, actually, as the right leg was still bent up like a stork's!) and off I went. I got to the window of the ward. Hooray and applause! Yes, there was life outside the hospital. In the park opposite people were enjoying the summer sun. The trees and flowers looked beautiful. I felt everyone was sharing in this triumphant moment. It was glorious!

'Do you think you can make it back to the bed or shall we get the wheelchair?' The physio looked a little concerned, but I could see Lynne's face urging me on, even though she couldn't speak (her vocal chords were in spasm) so I headed back to my haven. It seemed such a long way back. I was perspiring and breathing heavily. I must do it. I *must*. What a relief to slump down on the bed, but what joy that I'd been upright again for the first time in months! I'd been to the window and back. It was a marathon, but my heart and soul were dancing for joy.

For two days the improvement was steady, and the nurses were all commenting on the changes. I was sitting up without a collar, feeling brighter and stronger. Even though I was told the nasal feed drip would have to stay on for another fortnight, I was able to eat a few teaspoons of yoghurt as well, and was putting on weight. My brother Nigel had flown over from the States with Catherine after hearing I was at death's door, and they were amazed to find me so much better. There was even talk I could come home for a family reunion.

Then the setbacks started. The total body spasms, which had calmed down of late, returned with a vengeance. In one day I had four major body spasms, each one feeling as if my throat had a rope round it and someone was sitting on my chest. Everything seemed out of control now. My mind was reeling.

For so long I had held on to the belief that I would recover. I had thought I had crossed the last hurdle. Now it seemed as if there might be more to overcome. I was so, so tired. If only I could just sleep and sleep and sleep. Now and again over the next few days I wondered why I wanted to stay in this world anyway. Being with Jesus seemed far preferable to this cauldron of pain and effort. I knew I had little more effort to give.

Before it was too late I wanted to put one or two things in order. I asked Mum to get the florist to send two baskets of flowers to Mimi and Georgie with the simple message, 'I love you so much.' Both of us knew why I was sending them, but we made no comment, though Mum looked as if she was being tortured. When Annie visited me next, I tried to tell her that if anything happened to me, she could have first pick of my clothes! Then my thoughts turned to Amelia, my oldest friend. Even though she didn't share my Christian faith, there was a deep bond of love and understanding between us. She had gone off on a trip to the Far East in the spring, a parting which had been traumatic for both of us. We had both wondered if we would see each other again. On the last leg of her journey, in Bangkok, she had suddenly woken up in the middle of the night with a terrible feeling of panic and fear that something awful was happening to me. Rushing back to England as soon as possible, she phoned our home straight away — to discover that at the very moment of her panic, I was being taken into hospital. Amelia was now an actress, and while she was looking for work she was able to come and see me in the National frequently. She was a tremendous support. Even in the depths of this physical misery, she was able to make me laugh, and we relived many happy yet poignant memories of the fun we had had in our school-days. Her humour, warmth and vitality convinced me of one thing at least.

'Amelia, could I ask you to do something for me?' I asked carefully. Amelia nodded slowly, startled by my tone. There was a long pause while I summoned the breath to go on. I felt very weak. 'If I don't make it,' I went on quietly, 'would you look after Tom? He needs someone with a sense of humour like yours. But,' I added, trying to smile as my voice began to break, 'he doesn't like people who pick their noses!'

The sense that things were coming to some sort of finale was felt by us all. In the hours when I was conscious, I felt a great urgency to say all I had ever wanted to say to the people who visited me, and also to hear every minute detail of what was happening in their lives. My own life didn't seem real any more. Often I was so drugged that I wasn't sure if I was dreaming, or there really were people at my bedside. I was frequently confused.

One evening that week when Tom came in to visit me as usual, I exclaimed, 'Giles, how lovely to see you!'

And at other times, I was probably high as a kite. I felt animated, strong, even euphoric, despite my physical weakness. In those moments I felt so confident that God could do *anything* I frequently prayed out loud, without worrying who might overhear, whether visitors, nurses or other patients. And then I was brought back down to earth when something so trivial, like medicine stuck in my hair and all over my bed clothes which had to stay there until a nurse could come and clean me up, would remind me of my helplessness.

While Nigel and Catherine were over from the States, they both spent precious time with me. Catherine's mem-ories of our years as bright young starlets and then as professional dance partners, must have filled her with shock and horror as she beheld this crippled, emaciated body, particularly since the last time she had seen me I was perfectly well. Yet she overcame any repulsion, and during the days of her stay in England showed great love and tenderness, frequently getting right up into bed with me, despite all the tubes and the hideous nose drip. She spent ages brushing my hair which had once shone with rich auburn lights, and now hung lifeless and thin over my hunched shoulders. Hearing all the ballet news was like giving a thirsty person a long, cool drink, and I wanted to know all that she had been doing and seeing.

And yet, of course, it was torture too.

Catherine tells me that during these days I was sometimes distressed about my wasted body, and asked for pathetic reassurance that I still had dancers' calves. Catherine massaged my wasted muscles for hours and kept on encouraging me, but it must have been so painful for her, especially when I talked to her of one of my secret regrets about Mimi and Georgie if I died – that there would be no one to share with the children my passionate love of ballet. It might sound trivial, but I so much wanted to pass on to them that thing which had been of such importance and joy to me. Catherine understood that, and spent a lot of time getting to know the children better, inspiring them with her own passion for dance.

For dear Nigel it was even harder. Perhaps it often is for men. Catherine and I hugged each other and cried quite a bit, but he just looked on silently, his eyes betraying his agony of helplessness and shock. Afterwards he explained the irrational anger he felt that human beings should be allowed to suffer like this, all dignity removed. Six months before, they had had to put their dog to sleep, and privately he reflected bitterly that we treat animals better than we treat people. To him, apparently I looked like a Belsen victim, and he half-wondered (he admitted to me later) whether the kindest thing wouldn't have been to put a pillow over my head.

There was no way I was going to be allowed home for the family reunion and this left me very depressed. The full body spasms were coming thick and fast, and I felt like a tiny boat on a mountainous sea which might at any moment be swamped for ever by a wave or dashed on the rocks. Professor Marsden had been away on holiday, but when he returned at the end of June, the situation was again critical.

Amelia recalls best the day we call Black Friday. (In fact most days of the week were called Black at one time or other!) It was 30th June. She came in to the ward to see me, only to find the curtains drawn all round my bed and a lot of activity amongst the nurses. As she looked through the curtains, she found Tom and Professor Marsden discussing the very final, desperate resort – brain surgery. Then she saw me attempt a raw smile as I whispered, 'You're a hard man, Professor Marsden!'

Rushing out into the corridor, she bumped into my mother and just burst into tears on her shoulder like a child. '*How* do you cope?' she wept bitterly. I can only imagine my mother's suffering, gentle face, trying even now, at the last, to be strong for others.

A moment later Tom came out looking so unhappy, and all three were shown into a side room where Professor Marsden joined them, grave and compassionate. Quietly he explained the nature of brain surgery for Dystonia, an operation called stereotactic surgery which passes a probe with an electric current into the basal ganglia and, in effect, 'fries' those areas of the brain in charge of the abnormal movement. It is, quite obviously, a highly complex and dangerous operation carried out when the patient is actually conscious. It had only a 40 per cent chance of success. Damage and paralysis in other parts of the body are not uncommon, and Professor Marsden wanted us to be very clear of the risks and the limited nature of its possible success. Whilst the spasms might be stopped, it could mean that all normal function in that area might also be destroyed.

It was a horrifying decision for a husband to have to make. Now the full agony of the whole situation overwhelmed Tom. Amelia felt as if her own heart would break as Tom sobbed, 'I love her so much. I can't bear it for her,' while my mother, so small and beaten down now, reached up to try and comfort him.

'There must be something else we can do, Professor?' asked Tom desperately. 'I just can't let you do that to her.' But the alternative seemed only marginally less appalling, and no more hopeful. All they could do, the Professor explained patiently, was to knock me out completely with clonazepam, give me a tracheotomy, and put me on a ventilator, cabbage-like, for a week.

It was a bleak choice. When Tom came slowly, sadly, back to my bedside to discuss the dreadful decision, weak as I was, I had resolved not even to contemplate brain surgery. I think, in a way, that was quite a relief to Tom. But I pleaded with him just as desperately not to let them put me on a ventilator. I didn't want a machine to take me over, to be unable to communicate with those I loved, or even with God – for it all to end perhaps with the flick of a switch. We had been so sure God's healing had started. But where, where was He now?

8

The Treasures Of Darkness

'I will give thee the treasures of darkness ...'
(Isaiah 45: 3).

We would never have suspected that treasures were
hidden there, and in order to get them we have to go
through things that involve us in perplexity. There is
nothing more wearying to the eye than perpetual sunshine, and the same is true spiritually. The valley of the
shadow gives us time to reflect, and we learn to praise
God for the valley because in it our soul is restored in
its communion with God. God gives us a new revelation
of His kindness in the valley of the shadow. What are
the days and the experiences that have furthered us
most? The days of green pastures, of absolute ease? No,
they have their value; but the days that have furthered
us most in character are the days of stress and cloud, the
days when we could not see our way but had to stand
still and wait; and as we waited, the comforting and
sustaining and restoring of God came in a way we never
imagined possible before.

Anon

A decision had to be made quickly. The spasms were so
violent that there was a real fear that my neck would be
broken in the middle of an attack. But despite the horror

of the situation, several of us still had an obstinate feeling that we had already turned a corner – as if we knew a wonderful parcel had been put in the post but it hadn't yet been delivered. It seemed wrong to go and look for a replacement when the parcel might well arrive tomorrow. Besides, Virginia had told us of Jim Glennon's conviction that healing is often like a seed of corn: first the seed is placed in the dark earth, then as it receives rain and sun, so the blade appears, and finally the full ear of wheat. It would be ridiculous if the farmer ploughed up all the seed on the second day because it hadn't produced a harvest. Yes, it seemed as if we had already waited so long, but those closely involved were sure somehow that this was the eleventh hour. We mustn't give up now.

So in the end, a compromise was reached. The clonazepam dose would be increased further by drip, so that I was heavily sedated, but not so much that I needed to be on a ventilator. For about three days I was aware of very little and could barely talk, but at least there were no spasms. As soon as the drip was removed, however, the spasms returned, but doggedly we believed that their frequency and ferocity *would* grow less. There was an awful scare when pain started in the bottom of my lung, and pneumonia was feared. That would probably have been fatal, but it turned out to be a pulmonary embolism, a clot in the lung, dangerous enough in itself, but the threat was brought under control by a drip to thin the blood.

Gradually, gradually, I began to improve. Sometimes it seemed as if it was two steps forward and one step back, when a day without spasm would be followed by two huge ones the next. But we knew now, without a doubt, that we were on the home run. There was the wonderful pleasure of having my hair washed, of being helped into the bath, and then RED LETTER DAY, 11th July, when the nasal food drip was taken out. How wonderful to be a human being again, and not attached to any wires or tubes! I had to eat every quarter of an hour and was threatened with

The Tube again if I lost weight, but I was determined never to see that dreadful contraption again.

I was needing less and less of the relevant drug to bring the spasms under control, and a few days later I was told I could go home for the weekend if someone could do the injections. Tom was jubilant, and was given a bag of oranges by a doctor friend in order to practise giving injections! It was an act little short of heroic, but in the end my cousin Ginny, who is a doctor, was able to stay for the weekend. This proved just as well, for coming home in the car I had a violent body spasm, and they had to pull on to the hard shoulder on the Sidcup bypass while Ginny clambered into the back with the writhing beetle and gave the injection to knock it out until they got safely home. Over the weekend I was still very weak, but it was the best medicine in the world to be part of the family again. Tom's sister Kate was visiting from Australia, and on the Sunday she took a film of all the family group round our swimming pool in the garden. Feeling the sun on my white, papery skin, hearing the sound of laughter from the children in the pool, and the breeze carrying the scent of flowers up to the gently waving trees, I knew I would be well again. A week later I was discharged from hospital for good.

Although not instantaneous, my recovery from that point was dramatic. Within two weeks, I had thrown away my crutches on which I had been dependent for eighteen months. I was still very weak and the muscles of my legs, in particular the right one, extremely wasted, but I could walk unaided for short distances and was rediscovering the immeasurable pleasure of being independent again.

On 8th August I had an appointment with Professor Marsden. I was paraded in front of all his students and fellow doctors in the lecture hall and given a rousing cheer! In answer to Tom's question, the Professor admitted that in twenty-five years he had only seen one Dystonia patient who was as ill as I was recover. She was a lady who went to Lourdes and within a month of returning was completely cured. She had been 'in remission' now, as he put it, for seventeen years. So although the statistics for some sort of remission or improvement in Dystonia stand at 1 in 20 or 1 in 10, according to which source, it seems as if, in practice, total recovery from generalised Dystonia is very rare or almost unheard of. Professor Marsden himself underlined the role of faith in healing, not necessarily Christian faith but simply a positive belief by the patient that they would recover. In our close involvement now with the Dystonia Society, Tom and I have seen no other case of full recovery and we do wonder whether the statistics of remission are therefore published partly to give hope to those suffering from this desperate and bewildering disease. Anyway, Professor Marsden didn't hide his surprise and pleasure when he examined me, and commented to my GP on the 'remarkable improvement from the disastrous state' I was in previously.

My prime concern, now that I was getting better, was to come off the drugs as soon as possible. I was on a bewildering array of medication – tetrabenazine, diazepam, pimozide, artane, clonazepam, warfarin, to name but a few – all of which carried their own side-effects. I had been quite clear in my own mind that even if I were to have Dystonia for the rest of my life with whatever degree of disability, I wanted to avoid the side-effects of the drugs. I wanted to be *me* again, and to know exactly where I stood in my battle against the illness. But now we ran up against a new and very difficult problem. We hadn't really been aware of the highly addictive nature of some of these drugs. But around this time the evils of benzodiazepines in particular (which I had been prescribed for a long time) were beginning to be well publicised. The doctors had no choice but to prescribe these drugs if they were to stop me being killed by the symptoms of the disease – the violent body spasms and respiratory failure – but they must have known that if I recovered I would have an horrendous and almost impossible problem to deal with. I wonder, therefore, if they really thought I ever would get better and have to face the problem of withdrawal.

We took medical advice on how to come off the drugs, and made a long, complicated chart of the forty or so pills

I took each day, and the programme for cutting them out. Within days the horrible truth dawned. I was a complete junkie. As the drugs were reduced, so the indescribable aching and pain began. My body craved and cried out for the chemicals which had sustained it for so long. I wouldn't give in, and Tom was always there encouraging and supporting our decision. But this was only the start of the mental nightmare. Everyone around me was rejoicing at how much better I seemed. I was walking well and co-ordination was much smoother, but inside there was complete turmoil. I could see objectively that my body was responding correctly to brain commands, but somehow I couldn't appreciate my healing, or feel the joy I knew I should be experiencing. None of the pain of Dystonia or fear of death had ever brought blackness like this.

On top of these very real aspects of withdrawal, the terror, the anxiety, the restlessness, came the added psychological problems exacerbated by facing normal life after long, disabling illness. The most mundane details of everyday life suddenly seemed impossible tasks. I was unable, totally, to make any decision at all. The simplest problems brought great fear and a sense of terrible panic. What should I wear today? What should I eat for breakfast? Was it time to brush my teeth? It went on relentlessly all day. Decisions for myself were terrifying but if they involved the children they were just about impossible. And if I couldn't find some article of clothing for them, I would be overtaken by a blinding attack of panic, and turn the house upside down looking frantically for them before I realised an hour had passed and the children had long since gone to school.

The feelings of guilt, fear and inadequacy towards the children were probably the worst aspect of this time. I so desperately wanted to be a normal mother again, but it was hard to readjust to that role and establish a relationship once more with two quite independent children whom I felt I hardly knew. Independent, and yet at the same time so deeply in need of love and reassurance. I felt such a sense of regret and guilt at the three years of mothering I had lost, and a desperate urgency to make it up to them. Yet at every turn I seemed to fail.

When Mimi needed help with her schoolwork, I lost patience so quickly, or would stare blankly, uncomprehendingly, at the page of sums. Then she would retreat, crushed or bemused, and I felt terrible remorse that I was just driving her further away. Or Georgie's behaviour would seem so rude and cheeky, and I would either watch her flounce and pout, feeling frightened and helpless, or shout at her furiously, and be overwhelmed with guilt. Calm discipline seemed beyond my reach. Everything was out of control and out of perspective. I worried constantly about every small detail of their lives, as well as their schooling, their friendships, their development. I thought passionately about all the ballet, art, music, and craft I could be teaching them, and yet sat, paralysed with fear, in the kitchen when they came home from school.

In my brief moments of calm and lucidity, I was overwhelmed by the immense kindness shown by so many people every day. Tom's parents were so thoughtful, and with his sister, Polly, provided endless practical help and encouragement. Our nanny problems had been solved by the offer of a very special person called Melita who lived in the village, to assist with the children, driving, shopping and general organisation of the home. Melita herself has a son with a rare and disabling disease called Osteogenesis Imperfecta. Now in his teens, her son is a bright and determined young man, but as a family they have endured years of difficulties and countless operations. So Melita's thoughtfulness and efficiency kept the household together at times when I felt the whole pack of cards was going to crash down. My parents, of course, continued their unfailing support, and Mum often visited me, constantly encouraging and reassuring. Yet emotionally I was dead. Nothing moved me. There was no joy or sadness, just an emptiness filled with increasing fear.

So this was 'cold turkey'. My muscles began to twitch and jerk again, not from Dystonia, but from an intense longing for the drugs. I couldn't sit still for a moment yet wanted so much to have rest and quiet. My forehead was hot and damp, yet I was permanently shivering. Hot baths were a temporary relief and I had as many as eight a day to try to ease the aching. All feelings of time were out of proportion. A small task that would have taken a moment felt as if the whole day had passed, and then I had the terror of realising that only two minutes had gone by.

I crouched in the corner of the sitting room, my heart pounding and an overwhelming hurting in my chest. I struggled for breath, and fear invaded every part of me. Please don't leave me alone for a moment. Stay with me. Just hold my hand. Tell me there is nothing to fear. The children's chatter left me unable to move. Here were my two daughters, but they terrified me. I wasn't able to relate to them, love them, hold them, be with them. Yet I wanted all these things more than anything else. They must have been so muddled by their mother's strange behaviour.

Gradually the dulling, sedative effects of the drugs were wearing off and being replaced by feelings and emotions that had been suppressed for nearly three years, if not a lifetime. There was no rest. The nights were a jumble of nightmares, pounding heart, terrible blackness and overwhelming fear. God, where are you? You gave me the strength to come through so much, but now I feel abandoned. Jesus, where is the comfort and peace I know I can find in you? I turned repeatedly to the Psalms, holding on desperately to any words that could reach my drowning spirit: 'Wait for the Lord; be strong and take heart and wait for the Lord.' (Ps. 27:14)

I was waiting and waiting, but there was no peace. What do you want of me? 'For God did not give us a spirit of fear, but a spirit of power, of love and a sound mind.' (2 Tim. 1:7)

But my mind wasn't sound. It was wreaking havoc. And then the real thoughts of destruction. I became obsessed with my own death.

It was so much easier to get through the day thinking I would be dead by the evening. If I was talking to someone, I would be able to smile with the secret knowledge that my death was imminent. It was a good feeling, and excluded absolutely everyone else and what it might mean to them. I was very sick. For many days I would count out an enormous number of pills that I knew would be enough to prove fatal. I tried, feebly, to explain to those around me what was happening but never admitted the full horror of it all; my body was well now, so how could I put them through another round of hell? I withdrew from those who loved me. I knew this was the hardest time of all for Tom. After everything we had been through, it seemed as if he had lost his wife after all. Pale and drawn, he looked like a man bereaved. What should have been a time of rejoicing was turned into a time of mourning. He found my depression very hard to understand, and just once or twice, he rounded on me with some anger, and pleaded with me not to throw it all away when we had come so far. Desperately I tried to respond. Every time I failed.

During this terrible time, the only thing I had was God. There was absolutely nothing else keeping me alive and somehow from killing myself.

'The troubles of my heart have multiplied; free me from my anguish. Look upon my affliction and my distress, and take away all my sins.'

'Show me your ways, O Lord, teach me your paths; guide me in your truth and teach me, for you are my God and Saviour, and my hope is in you all day long.'

Again and again I read and tried to believe.

'Hear my voice when I call, O Lord; be merciful to me and answer me.'

My prayer was desperate and my spirit cried and ached for some comfort from the Lord.

There was a spiritual battle going on in my life that was so real I can only describe it as hell on earth. I had a loving, caring, husband, children, family, friends, home, but they meant nothing. All I had come through meant nothing. Everything people had done for me left me feeling guilty and worthless. I was now an able-bodied person *unable* to live. Friends and family came and went. The telephone rang incessantly. The doctor seemed to be here quite a lot. But it meant nothing.

One evening I did take a handful of sleeping pills. What joy at last. Peace. I had done it and it was so easy. Heaven would be so peaceful after this spiritual torment. But how quickly the moment of euphoria passed. What on earth was I doing? Tell someone before it's too late. A phone call. Tom. Then nothing. Sleep. How good to go to sleep. Shut it all out. Forget all this turmoil. A moment's remorse. Jesus. Hospital. Body spasms. More valium – probably the one drug that was giving me so much trouble. Lots of apologies. Feeling foolish. I'm sorry. I'm sorry. All drugs are taken away from me and locked in a cupboard. How foolish of me, but why hadn't it worked? Now my one chance of release had been taken from me and locked out of reach.

My one chance of release? Would God, who had worked so hard to bring me this far, abandon me now in the time of most desperate need? Would His healing, in the end, prove incomplete and inadequate? Those who had trusted God all this time refused to give up now. And gradually, into this lion's den of mental torment, He started to place angels of mercy and protection.

Just as the Lord had used friends such as Penny to give me strength and comfort at times of acute trouble, so He now drew someone else into my life as a channel of His healing. I first met Judy soon after I came out of hospital. The children were having a swimming lesson at a friend's house and I was watching from my wheelchair. Suddenly a slim woman knelt down by my side. Knelt, not stooped. Most people don't realise how much it helps a person in a wheelchair if they get down to the same level. Her face, which still somehow bore marks of suffering and sadness, was full of gentleness and warmth. We got talking and after a few minutes we were both aware of an unusual rapport between us, rather as two travellers from the same country might meet up by chance in some foreign city, and discover the pleasure of finding someone who speaks the same language. I wasn't surprised when she told me she was a Christian, and asked if I was, too. It was great to find a kindred spirit, and we chatted like old friends.

Over the coming weeks and months Judy was a constant source of encouragement through the mental torment of withdrawal. Married to Rodney, with five children, she had nevertheless had more than her share of heartache, and seemed to have an instinctive understanding of what I was going through. Time and again, she called at the house or rang me up just when things were particularly black, and kept encouraging me to hold on, that it all *would* get better, that I didn't need to try so hard. God accepted me as I was, she reassured me over and over again. I didn't need to meet any standard, either for Him or for the people close to me. Yet still I was driven on by this agonising sense of failure and guilt, the old spectre of performance and achievement returning to haunt me with the desperate compulsion to strive and strive in order to earn approval. Whether it was purely withdrawal from the drugs which caused these dreadful feelings of despair and inadequacy, or whether there was a further root of something still within me which had to be pulled out, it was hard to tell. But there was definitely some sort of barrier to the happiness I should be feeling as my physical recovery became daily more apparent.

The improvement in my mobility really was startling. Within weeks of being as twisted and bent as a hermit crab, I was walking tall and straight without any hint of a limp, even though my stamina and strength were still limited. Everyone was amazed and thrilled by the transformation, and the pressure began to mount for me to speak publicly about my healing. We agreed to host a barbeque lunch for the Kent group of the Dystonia Society, the thought of which filled me with panic as the date approached. Judy was able to talk me through the fear and help me to overcome it, whilst Annie, too, gave me untold support through these weeks. So aware was she, in fact, of my overwhelming sense of letting people down, of being a disappointment and a failure by being so miserable and crabby that she sent me a letter in which she actually quoted all the comments she had heard from friends expressing their love and support towards me, and included a notebook in which she urged me to write down all the bleak destructive thoughts so that I was at least getting them *out* and not pushing yet more hurt underneath. The diary makes painful reading now, but it did have great therapeutic value, and perhaps prevented the eventual act of desperation from being final. Judy also brought an elder to see me from the large house church in Sevenoaks she attended, and he, too, spent many hours over the coming weeks counselling me and praying with me. While I tried so hard to hide my wretchedness from most people, the love of these and a few others meant that I could throw away the act on occasions and let them see the hopeless mess underneath.

There was another group of people who also played a vital role in this aspect of my healing. As 'chance' would have it, in nearby Maidstone there is a very special group called The Blackthorn Trust. Founded by GP Dr David McGavin, it is a medical charity offering active treatment to those suffering from serious illness or debilitating life circumstance. But the uniqueness of the Trust is that it aims to understand illness in its whole human context and appreciates everyone's need to be understood and treated as having body, soul and spirit. It recognises that, when faced with an illness or tragic event in our lives, we often tend to regard it as an unfortunate accident, something that gets in our way and that we'd be a lot better off without! Illness can also make us feel like problems rather than people, and make our bodies seem little other than machines. Then we tend to think the doctor is the best person to take over the repairs when the machine breaks down. Dr McGavin believes that, viewed in this negative way, illness tends to diminish our stature. Our uniqueness as individuals can be overlooked and the great healing potential that we all hold within us is allowed to remain asleep. Instead of standing helpless and isolated on the outside, we should be at the centre, meeting the problem and gathering strength to overcome it. Illness, he feels, can then act as a challenge in our lives. No longer threatening to defeat us, but rather transforming and helping us find new direction. We, in turn, through our participation, can alter the course of our illness and also come nearer to accepting the fact of our own eventual death. While fully accepting the importance of surgery and powerful drugs, the Trust aims to extend the art of healing through natural medicaments, counselling, and the use of therapies – art, music, modelling, and movement therapy. By stimulating our life of feeling and imagination, these therapies promote new self-confidence, and enable one to move steadily away from being a victim of circumstance forward to the task of leading one's life with new enthusiasm again.

My own doctor arranged for Dr McGavin to come and see me at the end of August. The full force of the drug withdrawal was beginning to hit me, and I felt very low. I was dreading a visit by yet another doctor. But the tall, bespectacled man with the ready smile who came and sat with me didn't want to talk about me at all! Instead, in his hand, he carried a plant, still flowering but also beginning to produce its seeds. After an easy general chat we spent most of the first session trying together to be objective and appreciative in our observation of its lovely form, stage of growth and overall gesture. Looking back it does sound a bit unusual but at the time it had immediate beneficial effect in encouraging me to look outside my problem towards something positive, beautiful and alive.

I had many such talks with Dr McGavin. Not always about flowers! Sometimes we did talk about my illness and the present nightmare, but all the time there was the encouragement to view all the difficulties as keys which could open up positive feelings and new opportunities. He introduced me to other members of his team, and I started art therapy with Hazel – so creative and refreshing. The sessions were very structured and we were guided towards the development of positive emotions through the choice of colour and form. I loved the music and singing, and as the months passed I felt a growing strength. In Bons, a Dutch counsellor with the Blackthorn Trust, I found a real 'treasure in the darkness'. Apart from wisdom and compassion, she showed me so much love. In fact this characterised the Trust more than anything. There was deep caring for each individual. Everyone who came to the Trust found their worth as a unique human being infinitely reaffirmed. For many of us, illness had made us non-people, of little significance to the working of the world, with no confidence, little dignity and sometimes no hope. To the Blackthorn Trust, we mattered. Self-esteem was rediscovered, confidence grew. Lots of hugs and laughter gradually erased feelings of rejection and hopelessness. We blossomed – and then I understood Dr McGavin's flower.

But all this was still a long way off. The colours of autumn began to glow warm and rich, but the beauty still meant nothing to me. Perhaps I needed a complete break. Perhaps some excitement and fun would snap me out of this slough of despond? Tom and I duly booked into a small hotel in the West End for four days of the 'London Experience' as the tourist brochures call it!

It was wonderful to wander round shops and sights without being gawped at as a freak, and I managed to walk to Leicester Square, twenty-five minutes away, without any bother. Tom was thrilled to bits. Surely now his wife was back to normal? In a feast of culture we saw *Batman*, *Exclusive* (a play by Jeffrey Archer with my uncle, Alec McCowen, in a major role), *Rainman*, 'Mutiny on the Bounty' (an exhibition at Greenwich), *Blood Brothers*, and *Rejoice* (a play with Maureen Lipman) which seemed a fitting end to this celebration of my recovery. We rounded off our stay with a fabulous meal at Smollensky's and went to a Sunday service at St Paul's Cathedral. I hadn't seen Tom so animated and lighthearted for years. I tried desperately to smile and enthuse, laugh and chatter. But inside the fear and panic went on relentlessly.

Again I scoured the Psalms for comfort. Please, please God, don't let me go. I listened to the worship tapes Penny and Annie had sent, stared at the 'helpful' books left by thoughtful friends. Everything seemed meaningless. And again the thoughts of destruction. A fortnight later Penny arrived for the day with Edward, her youngest son and my godson. One look at me and she knew everything. All control and pretence had gone. I was at the very, very end of the line. But Penny, bless her, just refused to give up on me. We talked for a long time, and then, fighting to the last, she prayed against the thoughts of destruction, and banished the hold that 'Old Nick' had on my life.

Afterwards we both felt exhausted and walked the children down into the orchard. It was a really blustery day, and we stood and watched the little ones running about, enjoying the wind chasing them through the trees, the leaves blowing in great billows into their faces. Silently Penny and I stood together under the apple tree. Time seemed in suspension. Then, suddenly, I felt a great surge of power through me, a rush of warmth, light and freedom. I threw my arms into the wind and shouted, 'I've been healed!'

I *knew* it at last. Healed, not just in body, but right through, in my mind and in my spirit, too. We hugged each other and rejoiced at another victory for God. This battle was over. I had been released, I was certain from all the torment that had bound me for months. The enormous power and greatness of God, so evident in my physical restoration, had been revealed to me for a second time, only this time I was fully aware of it. I felt full of light, and very humbled by the absolute knowledge that God really did love me and care for me, even though I had wanted to end the life that He had given me. He had never given up on me either, even if I had almost lost hope in everything. I realised that God had always wanted to see me *whole* again, emotionally and spiritually, not simply out of a wheelchair and free from pain. The thoughts of death never returned. It was our tenth wedding anniversary. A new life lay ahead.

The change that came over me from that day was extraordinary. After all the years of pain and exhaustion, I was filled with tremendous energy and strength. I wanted to sing and jump and dance for joy. Dance! The muscles in my legs seemed to be restored very quickly so I found I could leap through the air with all the old ease and grace.

I whirled about the house like a musical tornado. The children, stunned by this transformation at first, quickly caught the feelings of celebration, and jumped and giggled and sang with happiness. In all my days of dance in worship, I had never felt or been able to express such depths of love and praise to God. I had discovered a well of happiness I didn't know was there.

Soon Tom, too, was able to believe that something big and wonderful really had happened, and that the nightmare was finally over. Our relationship, which had borne such wounds, was restored and strengthened with a deeper bond than ever. And so God's healing power moved outwards into the family. The atmosphere in our home was gradually filled with a peace and stability that we had almost forgotten existed, and the children grew calmer and more settled by the day. We were able to talk through all the hurts and fears, asking Jesus to heal their memories and fill them with His love. I knew that the process might take months, even years, but at least I could now cope with their insecurities and difficulties without feeling threatened or full of guilt.

By coincidence, Tom and I were invited to hear Jennifer Rees Larcombe speak at Tunbridge Wells just a couple of weeks after this incredible day. Jennifer, a well-known Christian author had been disabled by a rare viral disease and had been dependent on a wheelchair for eight years. The mother of six children, her continued disability despite all her faith and the prayers of those around her was particularly distressing, yet she was a beautiful, serene woman with an unshaken belief in God's love and power. I had read the story of her search for healing in her book, *Beyond Healing*, and now as I heard her speak, her face pale yet calm, my heart went out to her. After her talk I went up and spoke with her. I knew so well that she wouldn't want advice on how or what to pray – all I tried to do was encourage her not to give up. Little did we know that within a few months she would be dramatically and instantly healed, and telling her own story of God's intervention.

A few days later, I had a check-up with Professor

Marsden. Even he, with his measured, unemotional manner, was clearly more than pleased, and expressed his satisfaction in his letter to my GP:

> I was delighted to see Julie again today. She has really made a miraculous partial recovery from her very severe generalised Dystonia. What is responsible for this recovery, other than a spontaneous remission, I am not sure. She is delighted and so am I!

Evidently the medical profession, too, had had their reservations about the efficiency of all the drugs I was receiving, though I know they had to keep on trying with all the resources they had right up to the end. One or two of the doctors involved in my illness admitted to us later that, privately, they had just about given up hope. Hence, I suppose, Professor Marsden's use of the word 'miraculous', tempered immediately by the reference to 'partial' recovery (two fingers of my left hand were still painlessly curled up, a symbolic reminder of my illness). As one would expect, he attributes the healing to spontaneous remission. It would have been inappropriate for a doctor in his position to speculate publicly on any deeper cause. But we ourselves were in no doubt that my healing was divinely inspired, and that I was now kept in health by His power. Besides, I suppose there is an extent to which all healing, whether natural or supernatural (divine) is miraculous. The ability to create life, the power which causes growth and restoration, rest with God alone. It seems to me that the role of the doctors is to encourage and co-operate with this divine process. Doctors can set a bone and put it in plaster, but they can't *make* the pieces knit together; that is God's part. Doctors can cut out tumours, transplant organs, but they can't re-create a whole and perfect body; God can. So I am amazed and in awe of the wonderful, complex plan, the many channels, which brought about my healing, and I just praise God for the fullness and richness of the new life I have been given.

I was like a prisoner set free. Deprived of so many basic,

everyday experiences and abilities for three years, I found
excitement in even the most ordinary of situations. There
was such pleasure in being able to look at my wardrobe
each morning and choose 'proper' clothes to wear instead
of shapeless tracksuits which were comfortable to lie about
in. It felt good to be able to pull on normal shoes and
boots over feet and legs. I could put on make-up, style my
now-glowing hair. I was not only 'normal' again, but a
normal woman.

Throughout the illness I had been unable to drive and I
had found the restriction very hard. Now I went for a very
rigorous medical to test my fitness – and I almost kissed
the doctor when he told me I had passed! Oh the delight
of jumping (*jumping!*) in the car when I felt like it, picking
up the girls from school, dashing off to do the shopping.
This recovery of my independence was very important to
me.

Shopping – that was an eye-opener. On my first trip
alone to a supermarket in years, I couldn't believe how
prices had gone up. I spent a fortune! Like a child let loose
in a sweet shop, I wandered down the aisles picking items
off the shelves in a delirious haze of happiness. Everything
looked so colourful, interesting and exciting. After so long
trying to make shopping lists and menus for various nannies when I had lost touch with what was for sale in the
shops, it was marvellous to be able to choose meals *I*
wanted for the family.

To be able to walk, run and dance again was indescribable. After a lifetime of fitness and co-ordination, the disabling and debilitating aspect of my illness had been one
of the hardest to accept. From being carried slowly upstairs
for months, I was now taking them two at a time – and at
great speed! My body seemed to be overflowing with vitality, and I took up sport again. Tennis coaching was
arranged and I revelled in the fun of running about the
court and being able to co-ordinate movements again.
Swimming, too, brought the pleasure of feeling all my
muscles working properly once more, and healed the
memory of the agonising rituals of the hydrotherapy pool.

Even domestic activities were enjoyable. Previously I hadn't been able even to lift the lids on the Aga in order to cook. Now I could be as adventurous and creative in the kitchen as I wanted. Housework, as well, was fun (for a while!) reinforcing my independence in my own home. I was at the centre of my family once more. *I* was the one who played rough and tumble with the children, bathed them, walked out across the fields with the dog, organised the weed-pulling in the garden. In the quieter moments, it was lovely to lose myself in music – playing the piano or the guitar, and singing. Life seemed full of such rich opportunities and pleasures which I had taken for granted before.

Everyone kept saying, 'Don't overdo it,' but I couldn't help it! The excitement and joy of all these things was overwhelming, and each new experience highlighted the healing I had received. I would often get phone calls from friends. 'Are you *still* all right?' they would ask, and their voices would betray the anxiety they felt in case I wasn't. But I could *truthfully* say now, 'I'm fine. I feel terrific!' And gradually I once more became part of other people's lives too. Their fear that I would be whisked away again slowly evaporated. It felt good to 'belong'. Illness can make you feel very left out and lonely. It was fantastic to be able to join in everything again even though my heart did not stop aching for all those who continued to suffer from disabling diseases.

It was amazing how quickly the news of my healing got around. Our phone started ringing constantly with requests for my story. It began with an article in the local newspaper by a friend, Trevor Sturgess, then interviews on radio and television, and before I knew what was happening, it was in all the national press. By February I had also appeared on a couple of well-known TV chat shows.

I didn't find all this media attention easy. It wasn't the fact of the publicity itself. (If it had been for some dancing achievement I might have welcomed it!) But my healing was so recent, so personal – and in a way nothing to do with me. It was God who should be getting all the glory, not me. I didn't want to be treated like a celebrity, and somehow the slick, superficial way in which my story was portrayed seemed to sensationalise and therefore cheapen what was so precious and important.

One woman's magazine declared:

> Julie endured three years of pain and suffering during which she stared death in the face. But amazingly, just six months later she was totally recovered, *cured in just one hour by a modern day miracle.*

Nothing, of course, about all those who faithfully prayed and fasted, who encouraged and counselled, the dozens who, almost literally through blood, sweat and tears, never gave up hope. Nothing about the setbacks and disappointments. They made it sound like abracadabra.

It wasn't that I didn't acknowledge the vital role Jim Glennon had played in my healing. We all saw his visit as the trigger to my recovery, and I remain deeply indebted to him, not only for his ministry at that point, but his continued concern and support for us all. But he, too, shuns publicity of this sort, feeling that it is neither fitting, since it isn't his power or ability which does the healing, but God's, nor helpful, since it can make people seek help from *him* rather than the Lord. I had, in fact, done an interview for Australian TV live by satellite and the story had got into many Australian newspapers so that he was inundated with letters and calls from all over the world. Yet many people are healed every year through the healing ministry exercised in St Andrew's Cathedral, Sydney, where he is canon, without all this publicity.

The emphasis of the reporting, I feared, might have made people with chronic or life-threatening illnesses feel that unless they were lucky enough to meet a man with a 'miraculous' gift of healing, they didn't stand a chance, whereas the essence of what has happened to me is the faith, courage, perseverance, and love of ordinary people in frequently mundane situations. As the articles appeared, Mimi, especially, was very upset, even angry, at the way the role of the family, for example, seemed to be completely neglected. It even made her cross with Jim Glennon!

'*We* were the ones who prayed most, Mummy,' she declared passionately, and with some due cause. 'Every day we prayed, and we *never* gave up hope. THAT MAN only prayed for you for five minutes!' Her sense of hurt and injustice troubled me a lot, and we have spent a long time reassuring her of the power and importance of her prayers and faith. But it may not be until she is old enough to read this book that the whole complex yet wonderful web will be fully revealed.

Some people do have distorted views on healing. Once, after I had given a talk, a woman came up to me, and said, 'I must touch you, then maybe I'll be healed too!'

That sort of thing saddened and disturbed me. So when the suggestion was made by the publishers to write my own story, I welcomed the opportunity to set the score straight.

At first, as I mentioned at the beginning of this book, my instinctive reaction was to blot out everything about illness and disability from my mind. But before long, after tentatively sharing my own experiences with one or two bewildered people, I realised what a profound need there was for someone who had been through the terror, and had come out the other side, to pass on that hope. So Tom and I, and several others whose lives were deeply affected by my illness, have been very involved in the Dystonia Society in its efforts to educate the public about this terrible and not-so-rare disease, to provide funds for drugs and research into the elusive cure, and to provide support for sufferers and their families. Also, I wanted to help prevent others going through a diagnosis which implied the pain was 'all in the mind'.

There was one more thing I had to do. Tom and I had always promised each other than when I got better (when, not if, we used to say), we would have an enormous party by way of celebration, and as a thank you to all those who had supported us through thick and thin in such a variety of ways. We had never expected that we would be celebrating such a total recovery or so soon – and I could never have imagined that after being disabled and helpless for so long I would have the ability or energy to organise such a function. Yet I not only managed it but loved every minute of it.

We chose May 5th as the date, the day after my birthday, which added an extra air of festivity. It was just over a year since we moved to our new home, so it was something of a housewarming too. Two hundred guests were invited to our 'We're in the Pink party,' and through the genius of my brother Alec, whose business involves corporate and private entertainment, we transformed the lawn into a world of romance and fairy tale, with a beautiful pink marquee ballooning around the hanging baskets of pink and white flowers. Inside, the tables were draped with pink tablecloths, napkins, and delicate arrangements of flowers, and at the entrance an arch of about a hundred pink and white helium balloons formed an ethereal pathway into the fairy kingdom.

At least, I'm sure that's how it must have seemed to Mimi and Georgie. We all had special dresses for the occasion, and when the last ribbon was finally tied on each dancing, bobbing little girl, they both felt and looked like tiny Cinderellas – the more so as I had warned them they had to leave the ball at the stroke of midnight. (In fact they stayed up till long past one o'clock!) I, too, put on my Victorian-style dress of pink silk with hands trembling in excitement and anticipation. As I walked across the lawn with Tom, the evening seemed enchanted. The day had been hot and brilliantly clear. Now the night air hung heavy with the scent of honeysuckle.

What a spectacle lay before us. Gathered together in the marquee were all the people most dear or special to us – and all arrayed in the most magnificent attire of pink dresses, trousers, cummerbunds, bow ties . . . There was even someone with pink hair! The marquee was humming with the sound of animated chatter and people laughing. Quite apart from friendship and family ties, there was the common bond of involvement in my illness. Some had prayed, some had faithfully visited me in hospital, whilst others had simply left meals on the doorstep. And now we were all joined in thanksgiving for my healing, lending an even greater depth and poignancy to the sense of united celebration.

Tom and I owed so much to so many people, and it wasn't easy to give our short words of thanks. For my part, I simply reminded everyone how Tom had always been called 'the little miracle' by his parents because he was the only son amidst four daughters. As far as I was concerned that little miracle had grown up to become a big miracle, and without him there might have been no other miracle to celebrate that night.

The atmosphere was charged with emotion, and Tom heroically took over with a very funny speech which turned the tears to laughter. There was another difficult moment when he described the trauma of my final admission to hospital, but he rescued us all by recounting that brain surgery was eventually ruled out because they couldn't find my brain! Then he swept me on to the dance floor amid loud cheers and clapping.

We danced until dawn. As the darkness faded, we went outside and stood under the pink canopy of the early morning sky, the dew seeping through our shoes, refreshing our aching feet. For a few minutes no one spoke, then suddenly the sky was filled with balloons as the pink and white archway was cut loose.

Rising straight up on the still morning air, they seemed to all of us a kind of symbol – of past hopes and fears, of untold sorrows and hidden prayers. There was a sense of release, a letting-go. Another healing. For Tom and me, it was as if all we had received from God – our children, our friends, our family, our health, each other – we were now offering back to Him in thanks. The party was over, but a new life together had begun.

POSTSCRIPT

In August 1991 Julie went on a short retreat at Burrswood in Kent. There she saw a picture in her mind of a young woman in a pretty, new dress. Groups of people stood around her making comments.

The first exclaimed, 'What a beautiful dress you've been given. You lucky thing!'

The second grumbled, 'It's not fair! Why can't we have a dress like that?'

And the third muttered, 'Well, it looks all right from the front, but we can't see the back. It'll probably fall down in a minute.'

On closer inspection, the dress was found to be perfect but unfinished, with part of the hem still hanging down at the side.

As a result of this vision Julie received prayer, during which the two fingers of her left hand, which had remained curled in for the past two years, spontaneously straightened. Her physical healing, she feels, is now complete.

The Dystonia Society, a registered charity No. 326599, was established in 1983 to support sufferers of the neurological disorders known as the Dystonias which affect both adults and children.

Dystonia is an illness dominated by involuntary spasms of muscle contraction that cause abnormal movements and postures. It can affect virtually any part of the body, but commonly the neck, eyes or throat.

When Dystonia starts in childhood there is the strong likelihood that it will spread, leaving the child with a perfect mind in a twisted and contorting body, sometimes not even able to communicate.

It has been estimated that there are 38,000 sufferers in the UK although the figure is thought to be considerably higher due to difficulties of diagnosis.

The Society now has over 2,000 members with self-help groups and area contacts in many parts of the country who offer support to local sufferers.

For further information please contact the Central Office:

THE DYSTONIA SOCIETY
46–47 Britton Street
London EC1M 5UJ
Telephone: 0207 490 5671
Fax: 0207 490 5672

AFTERWORD

You have just read the story of Julie Sheldon and the graphic account of her illness and recovery. Our personal circumstances may be very different to hers but we can still identify with her anguish and that of her family, as well as with her worsening situation until all seemed to be lost. But it was when, in effect, they were saying 'this is the end' that there was this miraculous intervention. Many people can identify with that too as I can myself. St Paul said 'when I am weak, then I am strong'.

It may help to say that our problems do not come from God; they come from our corporate disobedience of God that the Bible calls 'the sin of the world'. Jesus has come in human form and taken away the sin of the world in his atoning death and has restored to us the Kingdom of God of which signs, including healing, are to be seen now. These signs are appropriated by repentance, faith and obedience. Because 'no flesh will glory in His sight' we draw on His gracious provision in a special way when we are at the end of our self-sufficiency (see 2 Cor. ch. 1, vv. 8–9). So Paul goes on and says 'I die (to self-dependence) daily'.

Providentially, I came on the scene when they were in this position and prayed a simple and informed prayer which believed Julie received healing so that I did not doubt in my heart (see Mark ch. 11, vv. 20–26). There can be great effect when outside and relatively objective faith is added to an inside and relatively subjective situation.

I hope Julie's story will encourage others to believe God for healing whether their circumstances are as serious or not as serious. I hope it will also encourage those who pray for others for healing to go further ahead in understanding and commitment.

JIM GLENNON
Sydney, Australia